BALLOTS AND BULLETS

Longarm had felt how hard the she-sheriff could punch with just her fist. So he wasn't surprised to see Duke Duncan crash through the whitewashed fence behind him . . .

Holstering his own gun, Longarm bent over to haul the unconscious bully out into the alley by his spurred boots, observing, "Tomorrow being sabbath you can likely get away with holding him clean through election day, Ma'am. That ought to make for the fair and orderly proceedings at the polling places I was sent here to assure."

She asked, "What if he still gets enough write-in votes to win?"

"In that case you and me had best be out of town before he's sworn in, Ma'am . . ."

*　　*　　*

This volume contains an exciting preview of *Sixkiller* by Giles Tippette! Follow the further adventures of the Williams clan in this new Western novel available now from Jove Books!

·→· TABOR EVANS ·←·

LONGARM

AND THE LADY SHERIFF

JOVE BOOKS, NEW YORK

LONGARM AND THE LADY SHERIFF

A Jove Book / published by arrangement with
the author

PRINTING HISTORY
Jove edition / May 1992

ISBN: 0-515-10849-9

Jove Books are published by The Berkley Publishing Group,
200 Madison Avenue, New York, New York 10016.
The name "JOVE" and the "J" logo
are trademarks belonging to Jove Publications, Inc.

PRINTED IN THE UNITED STATES OF AMERICA

10 9 8 7 6 5 4 3 2 1

Chapter 1

It was that socially awkward time after the fall roundup, with the evenings cool enough for all sorts of high-toned affairs in town and any number of ladies apt to turn up at the same one to fluster a poor cuss who'd meant no harm.

Deputy U.S. Marshal Custis Long of the Denver Federal District had no call to suspect Miss Irene Maguire of the Sells Brothers Circus of high-toned affairs. So Longarm, as he was better known by some, took Incredible Irene the India Rubber Girl, as she was known by many, to his more usual haunts, the usual number of times, with the results panning out a mite unusual.

Longarm's delight with a double-jointed redhead might have lasted way longer had not it been for professional courtesy. For they'd just done something delightful in her discreetly parked dressing wagon out on the fairgrounds and he was just lighting a three-for-a-nickel smoke to share betwixt the sheets with the lovably limber little thing when she coyly confided some circus-loving son of a bitch had swapped her a brace of front row center seats at the Denver Opera so's she could take in *Die Götterdämmerung* by Mister Richard Wagner, as sung by a posse of famous fat folk whose names she wasn't even about to to mess with.

Longarm went on setting his tightly packed cheroot aflame, running excuses through the loading chutes of a worried mind, while she toyed with the damp hairs

1

on his belly and intimated a gent who'd meant half the sweet words he'd just moaned in her ear whilst probing the depths of her womanhood with his insatiable shaft ought to be up to escorting a lady to just one teeny-weeny little opera.

He didn't think she wanted to hear how unfair it could be to hold any man to words uttered in ejaculation. He knew he didn't want to tell her where he'd been seated, with whom, the last time he'd been forced to sit through all that Wagnerian weeping and wailing. So he just stuck the lit cheroot betwixt her lush lips for her to puff on as he sighed and said, "I don't mind folk singing a tad off key in High Dutch and it was sort of amusing to watch all them gals in pink tights riding real brewery horses through fake clouds. But what day of the week might them tickets be good for, you sweet-bending belle of my balls?"

She laughed lewdly, cheroot gripped betwixt pearly teeth, and moved her free hand lower to toy with what he'd just reminded her of as she replied, "Saturday evening, when all the Denver swells will be there as well. I'm working the midway Friday night and all day Saturday, so's I'll be free to show off my new sateen outfit of kelly green to your stuck-up beauties of the golden West."

He'd been afraid she might say something that disgusting. He'd felt certain he was done for that time he'd spied Miss Morgana Floyd, Head Matron of the Arvada Orphan Asylum, from the private box of another opera lover. But, fortunately, the lovely brunette seated in the orchestra section had never glanced up to catch him hunkered in a box seat next to a way richer widow with way lighter hair while she, in turn, had felt no call to suspect a gent seated next to her instead of down yonder, where she could make out everybody, good, with those high-powered opera glasses she'd likely have with her every damned Saturday of the whole damned opera season.

Trying to sound as wistful as a blackjack player who'd just drawn a face card when he needed a deuce, Longarm tried, "I wish you had us tickets to say the Wednesday matinee, my pretty pretzel. For you know how much I cotton

2

to pleasing you in every way. But my cruel-hearted boss, Marshal Billy Vail, has me slated for some poll-watching up in the Wind River Country, starting this very weekend as a matter of sad fact."

It didn't work worth a mention. Sitting bolt upright in bed to shake one finger and both bare nipples at him, Incredible Irene let that lit cheroot go anywhere it had a mind to as she wailed, "Fibber, fibber, Indian giver! Why can't you just confess you'd be ashamed to be seen in polite society with a poor but honest freak-show girl?"

By this time Longarm had rolled off the far side of her fold-down bed to whip the top covers off before things could get any worse. The lit cheroot wound up harmless on hardwood in one corner of the compartment. He stomped the smouldering patchwork quilt with a horny bare heel and, when that failed to work, poured half a pitcher of wash water over it from the corner sink, muttering, "I never figured out just why that Miss Brunnehilde set her bed on fire in that other opera Mister Wagner wrote, neither. But for the record that fat lady sobbing and committing all that arson on stage ain't playing with real fire."

Incredible Irene pouted. "Don't try to change the subject. We both know Wyoming is still a territory, and even if they *were* fixing to hold elections in a territory they won't be holding any elections any damned where before the first Tuesday after the first Monday of next month, which will be November as soon as it gets through being October, you lying son of a . . ."

"Let's leave our kinfolk out of this," he cut in severely, as he left the damp bedding where it lay to lie back down beside her, adding, "I would never try to tell a well-traveled woman of the world a state election is about to be held up in the Wind River Country. But they're still holding *county* elections in them parts of the territory settled enough to incorporate into counties. The last time they tried for a fair and square election the federal governor had to send in a whole regiment. But this time the only position being hotly contested is for county sheriff, with the incumbent appointed to fill out the term of

3

an elected sheriff some poor loser dry-gulched summer before last."

He tried to ease her back down beside him. When that didn't work he placed a soothing hand in her naked lap and continued, "I know nobody will be voting for or against anyone for a spell, you pretty-but-too-suspicious little sweetheart. Marshal Vail holds, and I have to agree, it's tougher to *prevent* a rigged election after someone's gone and rigged it. He wants me to see if I can find out who might be up to something before they can get going, see?"

She started to move his hand from her privates but decided not to as she objected, "Pooh, you told me plain as day you worked out of that big federal building near the center of Denver. So even if some sheriff amid the wilds of Wyoming Territory *did* yell for federal help they'd have no call to send anyone like *you*. Don't they have any U.S. marshal up in Cheyenne, you big fibber?"

Longarm began to move two love-slicked fingers the way most gals liked as he told her, "It was Cheyenne as requested an assist from Denver because of the way the opposition party's been mean mouthing 'em of late. President Hayes replaced a heap of Grant's appointed marshals because they were crooks, but there was nothing in the constitution saying a Republican Administration had to pin all them badges on any Democrats or Grangers. So a certain number of country folk who've yet to forgive the Republicans for their picky attitude on the gold standard or shooting Indians out of season favor county governments of the opposite persuasion."

He got his fingers in as far as their middle knuckles and continued, "I disremember whether the incumbents would be Democrat or Grange up yonder. Either way, they've accused the territorial government of some sort of cover-up. So the federal court up to Cheyenne washed its hands of the dispute and requested Washington pick someone else to ride herd on the ballot boxes this fall."

She must not have wanted to hear the rest of it. For she suddenly sobbed and covered both ears.

With her bare feet.

This naturally caused her to fall backwards across the rumpled bedding. Longarm as naturally felt inspired to withdraw his fingers and roll atop her astounding display of ready, willing, and able anatomy. But as he sank his reinspired virility deeper than most gals could take it he felt obliged to groan, "Washington handed the hot potato to us because we were near at hand and used to police as far north as the South Pass when Wyoming was still Indian country. I sure wish they'd stuck Montana or Idaho with such a tedious chore. For I just hate to think of missing out on that swell opera with you this weekend."

She locked her ankles above her head and dug her painted nails into his bounding buttocks as she panted, "Stop fibbing about the damned future and fuck me deeper and faster in my here and now!"

That hardly seemed possible, but a man could only try to please a lady as best he knew how. So neither said another word for a mighty pleasant slice out of eternity and once they had come back down from the stars again she didn't seem to want to talk any more about poll-watching in Wyoming.

It was just as well. She'd have never bought him telling her who the Grange had nominated for county sheriff up yonder.

Longarm wasn't sure he bought it, himself.

The pay wasn't so grand but rank had its privileges and so in the normal course of events no deputy with Longarm's seniority would have been sent on such a kid chore. The Justice Department was always getting unsubstantiated complaints a new man could check out just as well, and Henry, the office clerk who typed up their travel orders, had said something about that kid who'd just transferred out from the Saint Lou District.

Thus it came to pass that Longarm got to work on time the next day, to the considerable surprise of the pale and skinny clerk he caught up with in the cold gray marble halls of the federal building.

Henry didn't unlock their office door. Nobody ever beat their mutual boss, the crusty Marshal Vail, to work. But he still felt obliged to ask, "What happened? Her husband came home unexpected?" as he opened the heavy oak door for the both of them.

Longarm smiled sheepishly and replied, as he followed the almost as tall but sort of wraithlike Henry inside, "She wasn't married and neither might at least two others be. But you're getting warm, old son. I've changed my mind about that poll watch up Wyoming way. So I sure hope you haven't already typed up them orders for anyone else."

Their boss hadn't lit any lamps in the reception room as he'd felt his way through the gloom to his own back office. So Henry lit a desk lamp as Longarm struck a match to get a wall sconce going. As it got lighter Henry said, "Surely you jest. I may be more ambitious than some people around here, but who'd prepare travel orders *that* far in advance? It won't be Halloween before the end of next week. So I was planning on some hunting and pecking oh, say next Wednesday. You're going to have to clear it with Marshal Vail if you want to go instead of that new deputy, Custis. I just work here and you know I'm not supposed to send you out of town just because you've gotten in Dutch with some gal again."

Longarm fished out a couple of cheroots and held one out to his fellow federal employee as he insisted, "I wouldn't be so anxious to see Wyoming this late in the year if I was only in dutch with *one* gal, Henry. As to it being a mite early, I was just telling one of the opera buffs I'd as soon not meet at the opera this weekend that crooked elections have to be planned in advance. So if I was to show up well before anyone expected me, and poke about for false notes as folk scramble to cover up . . ."

"Save such bedtime stories for your bedmates," Henry cut in with a knowing sneer as he put his own cheroot away for some sneaky future plans. "I thought we'd all agreed the cries for help came from a hysterical female so surprised by her unusual position in a man's world that she suspected all us men of ganging up on her."

Longarm smoked in public, like a grown man, so he lit his own cheroot, while Henry, moving around behind his desk to grab a seat, added, "You were back there with me

6

when Marshal Vail pointed out no clique of male county officials would ask Cheyenne to appoint a murdered sheriff's widow in his place unless they wanted her to *have* the fool job."

Longarm nodded, took a drag on his smoke, and declared, "It does seem odd she'd accuse three party machines in a mighty modest county of plotting her political downfall. But you got to allow any state or territory allowing women to hold public office has to have a mighty unusual constitution. Didn't New Jersey try letting women vote, one time, and didn't they decide it was a foolish notion and take the vote away from the little darlings a spell back?"

Henry, who had a whole rack of law books behind him, shrugged and said, "I think the women in New Jersey voted against the War of 1812 or maybe it was something about putting wife beaters in jail before they'd killed anyone. As of now Wyoming Territory is about the last place left where a woman could actually serve as such a high county official. One suspects the original mountain men up that way were so delighted to see the first few white women that they included them as civilized human beings against the more numerous members of the Lakota Confederation. But getting back to the here and now, Marshal Vail will never let me post you to that fool's errand over a week before a silly she-sheriff says they're fixing to screw her out of her job."

Longarm didn't want to study on screwing she-sheriffs. He was in enough trouble with gals who sounded less confusing, and he didn't think it wise to agree the lady they'd been talking about sounded sort of dumb. He was puffing thoughtsome on his cheroot, trying to come up with something more persuasive, when Marshal Vail in the flesh grumped out to confront them with his own stubby cigar puffing like a Shay locomotive going up a nine percent grade.

The somewhat older and way shorter and stockier Billy Vail slowed down enough to demand, "Are you just reporting in at this unwholesome hour, you lazy excuse for a federal employee?"

Henry knew their boss couldn't be talking about him, so he chirped right up in his teacher's pet way, "Deputy Long

7

almost beat me in this morning, Marshal Vail. We were just talking about that poll watch up in the Wind River Country. Deputy Long agrees with us that the widow woman charging mysterious enemies with being up to something mysterious could doubtless use a man about her house more than a deputy watching the ballot boxes for her."

The somewhat mollified Marshal Vail growled, "Damned A. I got better things for my deputies to do than to look under beds lonesome ladies suspect might be haunted! You know how come Cheyenne passed that case on to us, boys? They passed that case on to us because they know damned well there *ain't* no case, and I'm so mad I could spit!"

Suiting actions to his words, Marshal Vail removed the cigar from his fat face long enough to spit, and this time he almost missed the cuspidor near the umbrella stand by the hall doorway.

It was still a nice shot at the range, and Longarm said so as Henry insisted, "Deputy Long and me were just trying to figure some way to get shed of that pointless poll watch, Marshal Vail. For as you were only saying, yesterday, any fool woman who'd accuse others in advance of rigging an election would be certain to demand a federally supervised recount when, not if, she lost."

"Women!" grunted Billy Vail, sticking the wet end of the cigar back betwixt bared teeth as Henry soothed, "We were just trying to decide whether we could save ourselves a heap of bother by having someone run up to Wyoming well ahead of them even starting to set up the poll."

"To do what?" Billy Vail demanded with a suspicious scowl.

Longarm resisted the impulse to speak up when Henry seemed to be doing so fine and, sure enough, Henry said, "Run a routine inquiry and doubtless prove her charges have no merit well before anyone gets bogged down in tedious county-wide charges and countercharges, of course. What if we sent Guilfoyle, Smiley, or even Deputy Long here, to canvas a few party leaders on both sides just enough to . . ."

"I don't want to go up to the Wind River Country with winter fixing to beat me there!" Longarm cut in as he caught on, trying not to grin.

8

It worked. Their short grumpy boss snapped, "You'll go where you're damn well told to go and take along some wooly chaps if Wyoming in Indian Summer is too cruel for your delicate complexion! I got some courthouse chores for the better-dressed Guilfoyle, and Smiley scares folk better than he might canvas 'em."

"But, Boss—" Longarm couldn't resist sighing as Henry had to look away, inspiring Billy Vail to draw himself up to almost medium height as he growled, "But me no buts and get up to Wyoming on the double before that fool woman has Washington sending in the Seventh Cav!"

He told Henry to get cracking on the standard six-cents-a-mile onion skins and Henry managed not to laugh out loud as he said he'd have Longarm on his way in no time.

Vail said, "Bueno. I'm late for a meet up with Judge Dickerson down the hall. So you boys take care of that infernal she-sheriff for me."

He got as far as the doorway, paused there, and couldn't resist suggesting, "Maybe you can cure her of what's ailing her, Custis. Many an old widow woman has been restored to sanity by no more than a good stiff pronging, and that could be all it takes to close this case."

Then he stubbed out, slamming the door behind him before Longarm could ask what that she-sheriff up Wyoming way might look like. So he turned to Henry with a grateful grin and said, "You're all right and not half as dumb as you look, Henry. Do you want me to ask her if she has a friend for you?"

Henry grimaced and replied, "Not hardly. Any friends of a hysterical widow running for sheriff would likely be as mean and ugly."

Chapter 2

Getting there was half the chore. The Wind River Country lay sort of lost amid the higher half of Wyoming Territory, which was remote to begin with. No rails ran within a hundred country miles of where he had to get to. So Longarm dropped off a U.P. combination at Fort Steele, where they had to jerk boiler water from the headwaters of the North Platte in any case.

He got off wearing the tobacco tweed three-piece suit they made him wear on official government business. But knowing how long he'd be alone on the trail in mighty lonesome country he'd packed some well-busted-in riding duds, including a sheepskin mackinaw and goatskin chinks, or kneelength chaps, to wear over clean but threadbare blue denim when, not if, the autumn winds shifted less friendly.

As an experienced High Plains rider, Longarm knew spring and fall were the times of the year Mother Nature, or Old Man Coyote, liked to pick off greenhorns with hundred-degree temperature swings—either way.

The weather had been about right, so far, since a nicer-than-usual greenup. Folk out this way who knew them said that was the time you could expect Mother Nature or Old Man Coyote to spring a Halloween blizzard or a Thanksgiving heat wave. Holding elections in November made way more sense back East.

The remount officer at the dinky cavalry post didn't want to outfit a civilian working for the same federal government with a couple of ponies until Longarm explained over drinks in the post canteen how he'd been stuck at another post one time by other horse hogs until, seeing he'd had time on his hands and no place else to go, he'd uncovered some mighty interesting irregularities.

His new pals at Fort Steele sent him on his way with matched army bays they'd let him pick personal from their remuda. They were both geldings, each a couple of hands taller than your average Indian pony. There hadn't been any serious Indian trouble up this way so far, this year, but a man still felt a shade less worried in the company of well-shod and oat-raised cavalry stock. For no matter what that old French cuss wrote about the noble savages he admired so much, it simply wasn't true that Indians had better horses and knew more about the same than the race who'd invented horsemanship three thousand years before the first plains Indian, likely a Comanche, laid eyes on his very first horse, or "spirit dog," as some nations still called the critter.

Longarm rode out to the north from Fort Steele the next sunrise, riding the bay he'd saddled with his old army McClellan for no better reason than that he'd already put his packsaddle on the other. He'd given himself no more than four or five days on the trail, tops. So the pack brute wasn't loaded with a full hundred pounds of possibles. That allowed him to set a fair pace, forging on after swapping loads. He was more concerned about the lateness of the season than he was about getting there, or someone trying to stop him. But the day that had greeted them so crisp-but-clear stayed friendly as, if anything, it warmed up to swell riding weather.

The so called Wind River of Wyoming Territory ran northwest to southeast as a broad-braided stream along the aprons of the no-bullshit Wind River Range, a serious section of the Continental Divide, but you couldn't tell how high in the sky you might be as you first rode out from Fort Steele. For even though the tawny swells of sun-dried grass all about were officially mapped as a part

11

of the Rocky Mountains, the granite spine of North America had somehow wound up under a whole lot of softer dirt in *these* parts. So they called it the Great Divide Basin, even though it lay more than eight thousand feet above sea level and greenhorns crossing it on the transcontinental trains got headaches and saw stars with their eyes shut because of the thinner air. It was the even higher country all about that qualified this stretch of the Great Divide as a *basin*. Sort of. Water still ran from the draws all around to the Atlantic or Pacific, depending.

It took more than a change of saddles to rest a pony after half a day on any trail. So along about noon, finding himself and his ponies near a wash-fed lake somewhere betwixt Fort Steele and Camp Ferris, he unsaddled both brutes and hobbled them to water and graze as they felt fit along the marshy shoreline while he took time to brew himself half a pot over a modest fire of dried sage and rabbitbrush.

Earlier travelers had gleaned the last buffalo chips left over from what the Indians wistfully called "The Shining Times," and nobody seemed out to raise beef this far from civilization, yet.

Longarm was just as glad. As he hunkered by the fire in his sun-faded denims, admiring the distant lavender ridges of the Seminoe to the northeast, it felt easier to imagine what this country had been like way back when, before the Mountain Men or, as long as he was dreaming, before the first human of *any* breed had come searching for something worth messing up.

Longarm was fair-minded enough to include Indians as members of the human race. So unlike some, both red and white, he knew the only reason noble savages had left so much for everyone else to despoil was that they hadn't had the time and tools to kill all the game, cut all the timber, and shit-up every fished-out trout stream.

He'd hunted buff with Indian pals. It was true they didn't take as many, when they couldn't find a cliff to run the whole herd over, but it had never been for lack of trying. Buffalo rounds were expensive, even for white hunters, and old Mister Tatonka took a spell to drop with no more than a couple of trade-tipped arrows in his shaggy chest.

"I wonder how come I'm thinking so much about Indians," Longarm muttered half aloud as he was opening a can of pork and beans. The troopers back to Fort Steele hadn't issued the usual warnings about young bucks prowling off the reserve for easy brags, this autumn.

He was a good piece from the nearest reserve in any case, and that'd be, right, the Shoshone Agency up to Fort Washakie. That bunch had stayed friendly during Red Cloud's War, and the Shoshone rising of '78 had been a tempest in a teapot, inspired by Custer's misfortunes on the Little Big Horn and asshole bragging on the part of both red and white assholes, afterwards. The Washakie Shoshone had tried to stay out of it. Only a few of their young men and a band of Arapaho malcontents off the same reserve had jumped the same. Longarm wasn't sure he'd want to be posted to a Shoshone Agency if he'd been born an Arapaho, either. The two nations had about as much in common as say Scotchmen and Greeks. But to the Bureau of Indian Affairs an Indian was an Indian.

Longarm finished opening the can and set it aside to wait up for the Arbuckle as he fished a cheroot from his denim jacket and poked a straw stem in the fire for a light. Then he decided he'd rather have his sense of smell unimpaired as he muttered around his unlighted smoke, "If I don't smell me an Indian I'm commencing to grow me a sixth sense, like that Madame Blavatsky who wrote all that stuff about communicating with the Great Beyond without no telegraph line."

Keeping his hat brim low above his shaded eyes, Longarm scanned far as he could, both ways, without moving his head. He and the two hobbled ponies seemed to have the calm lake and rolling grass beyond all to themselves: no Seminoes peeking over the horizon at them. One of the cavalry mounts was swishing its tail more than the noonday dearth of flies at this time and place seemed to call for. But both brutes would have been acting up more than that had they noticed other ponies close enough to nicker at.

Longarm was in the habit of tethering riding stock a ways out to pussyfoot the rest of the way in, himself. He poked

13

at his fire with a hardwood stick. The pot was commencing to simmer now, and the coals he had going were likely enough to finish the chore. But he still rose wearily to move out just a ways and bend over to grab hold of another clump of summer-killed tarweed.

Everyone knew dried tarweed burned swell. The cuss flattened out behind a clump of soapweed atop the rise to the south must not have known how fat his blue-clad rump had grown since last he'd taken such skimpy cover. Longarm ambled back to his fire, hunkered down again facing inconvenience for the stranger watching him from that rise, and let the tarweed blaze between them as he casually reached across his own lap for the cross-draw grips of his double-action .44-40 and called out, "Coffee's about ready and I can always open another can of beans if you'd rather visit than fight."

There was no answer.

Longarm tried, "I'd be U.S. Deputy Custis Long on my way to Camp Ferris, come sunset and the creeks don't rise. I'm packing no warrants on anyone I know of in these parts and I am talking to that fat-assed soul behind yonder soapweeds atop that rise no more than fifty yards or a tolerably tough pistol shot from here. So what's it going to be?"

The Indian who'd been scouting Longarm from the soapweed rose sheepishly to a modest height, calling down, "Don't shoot. My nation is not at war with your nation. I am Absaroka or what you Wasichu call Crow. I don't know why. Absaroka means Sparrow Hawk Person. We used to be the Sparrow Hawk Clan of the Hidasta you call Sioux. But *they* didn't understand us, either."

It was Longarm's turn to look sheepish as he called back, "I'm sorry I implied your derriere was more than ample and I can see why you felt shy about a strange Wasichu just now, ma'am. But I meant what I said about coffee and beans, before."

The somewhat chubby but otherwise young and pretty Indian girl replied she had to see to her own pony's comforts before she might her own. Longarm nodded approvingly but didn't put his six-gun away before she reappeared atop the

14

same rise with a plump paint in tow.

Sensing they both had healthy appetites, Longarm moved over to his nearby packsaddle to break out more beans and, hell, some tomato preserves, as the pretty little thing unsaddled, watered, and hobbled her own mount to enjoy the lakeside scenery with the army bays.

As she joined him by the fire he refrained from sniffing obvious but he could still tell she had a tub bath with real soap and splashed plenty of violet toilet water over herself as well within, oh, say a week at the most.

Her tailored trading-post riding habit, just a mite too rustic to call fashionable, was cut from the same practical— but newer, and hence bluer—cotton denim. The lighter-blue man's work shirt she wore under the waist-length jacket looked too clean for a full week on the trail. So how come he'd smelled Indian, at that range, when she seemed clean enough to take to church, up close?

He was still alive, with all his hair, because unlike a certain George Armstrong Custer he'd always gone with his first instincts when it came to Indians. So he kept his guard up as he sat her down in the dry grass beside him to serve her some coffee and trail grub. When he apologized for the strong black coffee she dimpled sweetly and said her own folks had never served it with white flour in it, Indian style, either. He wasn't surprised when she went on to say her folk had been mixed bloods, Crow and French Canadian, who'd served as licensed traders and translators up Montana way.

That seemed to explain her tidy duds and toilet water as well as other features more in keeping with Victorian standards of beauty. It didn't ease his mind worth mentioning about his earlier suspicions about Quill Indians scouting him.

He'd naturally put his gun back in its cross-draw rig by then, but the hairs on the back of his neck just refused to calm down as he deliberately leaned closer than he needed to, pouring her more coffee, and inhaled downright rudely, judging by the way she sighed and said, "I took a good bath the night before last and changed my unmentionables this very morning. It must be something bred in our bones.

I could tell you were Wasichu if I met you in the dark, too. So don't be so stuck up about it."

He sighed and assured her, "I ain't. I've met lots of your kind in the dark, right friendly, and it ain't in our bones. It's more what we eat, drink, smoke and scrub down with. At the risk of insulting you further you smell just as good, or just as bad, as your average white gal, Miss . . . Ah?"

"Marie, Marie Mato Wastey or Good Bear in Wasichu." She replied rather primly, adding, "I don't smell like you at all. You smell of sugar cured tobacco, bay rum, naptha soap and . . . man."

He smiled thinly and said, "I had a cold-water wash off early this morning and I meant you surely couldn't have been what I got a whiff of, earlier, at that distance. It's none of my beeswax where a part-white and entirely peaceful Absaroka might be headed, Miss Marie, but are you certain you've been traveling alone from wherever to wherever?"

She washed down some beans with Arbuckle as she nodded innocently enough, then said, "I've been traveling alone on delicate but perfectly lawful family business. Our agent at the Big Horn Agency knows I'm running wild in my feathers and paint down this way."

He chuckled, washed down some of his own beans with the tomato preserves lest they run out of coffee before she'd had her fill, and said, "I just now said I wasn't interested in that part. There's this Madame Blavatsky who just moved to East India, from when she issues instructions on reading minds, finding Lost Atlantis and such. But I ain't sure I can go along with her on every revelation and even if I did have uncanny unsuspected powers it couldn't have been a well-mannered young lady from a friendly nation I sensed creeping up on me just now. Seeing you'd be Absaroka, it's safe to let you know I've tangled with less civilized nations all up and down these Shining Mountains and I saved my hair more than once by ducking sooner than I'd figured out just why."

The Indian girl moved the tin cup downwind from her flaring nostrils and waited a spell before deciding. "The only sweated-up stranger I can smell around here would be *you,* Deputy Long."

He sighed and said, "Aw, I ain't so strange and you can call me Custis, Miss Marie. But hold the thought and keep an eye on things here as I scout out around us some. I got a derringer, here, you can hold in your lap 'til I get back, seeing you left your bow and arrows to home."

She calmly raised the hem of her split skirt high enough for him to spy the pearl-handled Allen & Wheelock .25 strapped to her right boot as she demurely replied, "I'm a long way from home and could anyone be *that* young and innocent?"

He chuckled, rose to his feet, and ambled over to the McClellan he'd lain upside down in the grass to dry as he called back to her, loud enough to be heard a good ways, "Well, all right, if you're just bound and determined. But I still say high noon is a mighty poor time to pot anything worth supper!"

She was either too smart or too confused to yell any dumb questions back at him. So he simply bent to draw his Winchester from its saddle boot as innocently as any other rabbit hunter might before he strolled in the general direction of the highest rise within a mile or more.

It didn't work. By the time he was high enough to have Marie and the three ponies almost as little as grasshoppers, somebody else had ridden off to the west, alone and lashing his mount some, judging from the faint dust against the otherwise crystal-clear sky over that way.

He went back down, scooped up his own saddle and bridle to inform her as they both ran over to the ponies along the lake shore. "I told you there had to be less friendly Indians around here. I make it one. Likely scouting for a bigger party. Your turn."

She said, "I've no idea. I thought this was Ute or Shoshone country and neither have their paint on this summer. What about Arapaho? You can never tell what Arapaho might be up to. My elders say not even an Arapaho can tell you what is in his heart, because Wakan Tonka made the lying dogs *without* any hearts!"

By this time Longarm had the nearest bay bridled. He

said, "Hold these reins whilst I saddle up if you want to be useful, and farther along, as the old song says, we'll know more about it."

She said, "Saddle your own tashunka. I'm riding with you."

He started to tell her she'd be safer staying put. Then he wondered why anyone would say a dumb thing like that and grunted, "Wastey! Let's get cracking before the stinky bastard gets away!"

Chapter 3

The stinky bastard got away, partly because of common sense. It was Marie who asked whether it felt wise to leave that other army bay and all those trail supplies unguarded. But Longarm had already commenced to think back on his Indian scouting days during the big scare of the seventies. So with the help of a friendlier Indian he broke camp proper and left nothing by that lonesome lake for anyone to lift when or if they doubled back on any trail one might follow across soil baked firm as wall plaster.

Their mysterious stalker had started out to the west north-west as if beelining for the center of the vast so-called basin. Marie had to take that on faith by the time they reined in atop another rise a mile west of that lake for another sweep of the far horizon. For the cloudless cobalt-blue sky met the rolling sea of shortgrass straw in a razor-sharp and clean-as-a-whistle line.

Longarm muttered, "I just hate it when a rider notices how much dust he's raising and slows down. He has to be somewhere out yonder. But as Custer and his boys found out, one time, you can tuck a whole blamed tipi town in any one of the gentle but serious dips in rolling prairie, open as it looks!"

Marie murmured, "Why are you telling *me* this? Didn't I just tell you I grew up on the high plains of Montana Territory? If that rider you spotted was scouting us for a war party *we* are the ones who ought to be down off the skyline right now."

Longarm nodded soberly but said, "The odds are greater he was out to steal ponies, or maybe you, on his lonesome. Quill Indians out on serious mischief don't have lone scouts out that far and hardly ever run from two potential victims, even when both of 'em are grown men, no offense."

She sighed and said, "I wish you'd stop lecturing an Absaroka on local customs. Since we're on the subject, you've heard of the prairie plover's broken wing trick?"

Longarm had. He chuckled dryly and replied, "Some say Custer fell for that at Little Big Horn. It's tough to be certain when there are no survivors. But if that lonesome polecat somewhere out yonder was trying to lure us into an ambush by just pretending to be alone, how come he'd been riding so shy? That dispatch rider Custer sent over to Benteen's column, lucky for him, reported Custer and his command were in hot pursuit of a manageable war party. Old George never would have taken on better than ten-to-one odds had he known what he was really up against. But on the other hand he'd have never led his column after nobody at all and, as of now, I don't see nobody at all out yonder."

He nonetheless heeled his mount down the far slope, muttering of the time he'd scouted Shoshone, not too far nor long ago from there. She didn't ask what he was searching for in the dry thatch all around. They both knew that while unshod ponies left no hoofprints in springy sod a good six or eight inches thick, they still dropped horse apples now and again. It was easy to read how recent, with the few fall flies so thirsty.

It was Marie who reined in and slid gracefully from her saddle to drop to one knee, calling out to him. By the time Longarm had turned back to rein in closer the Indian girl was back on her feet, holding up what looked at first to be a snake she'd caught by the tail.

He recognized it for what it really was before she announced, "You were right about him being sort of backward. Look at this boasting braid he had woven into his real hair!"

She didn't have to tell a man who'd scouted in the seventies what a boasting braid was. Quill Indians set great store by the length of their hair. Save for Pawnee, who favored sort of Mowhawk haircuts, most of the plains nations agreed with Samson in the Good Book that luxurious uncut hair was Wakan Wastey or Good Medicine. Like white folk of both genders they were not above improving on nature and other Indians, a people possessed of a certain dry sense of humor, dubbed the results "bragging braids."

Holding the one she'd found up to the sunlight, Marie declared, "He was wearing his paint as well. Traces of yellow and green, maybe blue, rubbed off by this hair as it whipped him across the face before breaking loose."

Longarm turned in his saddle to gaze back the way they'd come as he mused aloud, "Well, that dust I spied from way over yonder might have been rising from way over here and having things fall off as he whupped his pony might have restored some common sense to him. So the question before the house is which way did he go from here, at a more cautious pace?"

Marie tossed the two-foot length of braided greasy hair away and bent to wipe a palm fastidiously on the sun-baked and wind-washed grass as she absently decided, "Lakota, like my own people, almost always have some red paint on when they're cross with someone. Cheyenne like blue, black and yellow. Black wouldn't show against black hair. Yellow is wakan wastey to most of the nations. So it depends on whether those few hairs had rubbed against blue or green."

As she remounted her paint Longarm decided, "Arapaho use green more than anyone else and we're just too far west for Cheyenne, even if they were on the prowl this fall, which I'd have heard about."

She said, "We heard about all the Wasichu the Cheyenne scared down by Denver that time. I just told you Arapaho turn up anywhere, doing anything. They fight more like *shunka*, I mean dogs, than real men. I have never heard of them taking the warpath all by themselves. Have you?"

He frowned thoughtfully and replied, "Come to study on it, Arapaho do seem to get in more trouble riding with other Indians. There were Arapaho backing or just visiting Cheyenne at Sand Creek and Washita. None of the

Arapaho at Little Big Horn were in charge and, now that you mention it, the Shoshone up north of here have some Arapaho sort of roaming with 'em. Some say they was adopted by that friendly Shoshone chief, Washakie, whilst others say some B.I.A. pencil pusher just failed to find a better place to pigeon-hole 'em and figured the Washakie Shoshone were less likely to hurt 'em than your average Wyoming cowhand. Either way, that's the nearest band of Arapaho and, what the hey, I'm heading up that way in any case. The white agent up to Fort Washakie ought to know whether he's missing potential trouble in serious numbers. If we're just talking about a lonesome horse thief I got bigger federal fish to fry."

She agreed they'd doubtless seen the last of the rascal neither of them had really gotten a good look at, unless he doubled back to attack them with a whole war party.

Longarm grimaced and said, "You'd best stick with me 'til we find out, Miss Marie. I was planning on spending the night at Camp Ferris. Doubt I'll make her before nightfall, now. Where might you be headed, if you don't mind my asking?"

She sighed and said, "Casper Ferry, where the old Oregon Trail crosses the North Platte. I have been trailing a naughty kid sister all over this country and they just told me down in Rawlins that she'd taken up with a Metís who used to run a trading post at Casper Ferry."

Longarm whistled softly, trying to gauge how much of what she might have in the saddlebags and bedroll of her center-fire stock saddle.

He soberly decided, "You must be anxious indeed to catch up with her and her Canadian breed, then. Casper Ferry has to be a hundred mile crowflap from here, on the far side of some serious hills. That's way out of my route to the north but I can see you safe at least as far as the Seminoe Range beyond Camp Ferris to the northeast."

She nodded gravely and said they'd surely be caught alone on the trail by nightfall and mayhap worse if they didn't get cracking. So Longarm decided to swap mounts later, after they'd put some distance between their real scalps and that discarded boasting braid.

Longarm was curious as anyone else might have been about what seemed a juicy family scandal. But since he wasn't a member of the Good Bear family he'd have sounded curious as an old biddy hen if he'd asked right out about it.

So he never. It hardly seemed possible a kid sister running off with even a dirty old man could qualify as a federal offense and Billy Vail sure frowned on his federal deputies righting lesser wrongs on the taxpayer's bought-and-paid-for time.

He'd found most women tended to share family secrets, sooner or later, with fellow travelers who didn't press 'em. So he didn't press her and farther along, bit by bit, as he shared his tobacco and water with her, a not-too-pretty picture of a pretty kid sister, fifteen summers of age but at least as experienced as Madame Moustache down in Dodge, began to emerge from the mists.

He was too polite to ask Marie why she or anyone else at her Crow Agency wanted such a tiresome child to come home. There was something about a hard-working gent back yonder giving lots of presents and blowing lots of sad songs on his nose flute only to have the little sass mock him, insult him, and even worse, sell the riding stock he'd really bestowed on her elders to white cowhands she'd apparently sold other favors to as well.

The more he figured out, the less Longarm wanted to know about a mighty sticky situation the B.I.A. was better fit to cope with if things reverted to old-time Absaroka customs. Crimes of passion were dealt with on a case-by-case basis, and most Indians were left alone to sort things out. It wasn't true, as some might hold, that noble savages lived free under the natural laws of their own good natures, unsullied by the corruptions of civilization. Longarm was dead certain the French philosopher who'd come up with that odd notion had never witnessed a sun dance or been there when war prisoners were turned over to the women and children. An outraged lover usually settled for simply beating a false-hearted woman to death with anything handy. It was up to the older women, and how they explained it all to the dog soldiers, whether he was punished or not. The dog soldier lodge just kept order in the band. Public opinion of the few who got out of order determined what the dog soldiers might or might not do about 'em.

Longarm was able to shift his load from one bay to the other as the sunny, almost warm afternoon wore on. But since Marie only had the one mount they were forced to take longer trail breaks than he'd planned on. The Indian girl, alone, couldn't have weighed more than say a hundred and thirty, bless her plump hide, but the Indian pony she said she'd picked up in Rawlins had a harder-than-usual row to hoe with her riding as well as full-figured.

Along about five that afternoon, with the late October sun still limelight-white in the thin dry air but getting sort of low to the west by now, Marie said there was no sense pushing their poor ponies so hard because they were never going to make it to the next town in any case and that, really, she didn't mind sleeping under stars on top of grass with the weather this dry.

He nodded but said, "You got to worry about bed bugs in trail-town hotels in any case. I got plenty of coffee and grub, as long as nobody expects nothing fancy, and my own bedroll's waterproof as well as warm enough, this side of the Blue Norther. But let's keep beelining for Camp Ferris anyway, in case anyone's still scouting us with all that swell sun-glare backing their play."

Marie gulped and almost glanced back to their west, but remembered some lore of her wilder cousins in time to nod soberly and decide, "Wastey. If they think we are anxious to get to the only settlement for many miles they won't circle to lay for us anywhere else."

It had been more a statement than a question. Longarm still nodded and said, "That's about the size of it. If they were figuring on a running gunfight they'd have commenced chasing us cross open country by this time. But as anyone can plainly see there's a heap of open country in all directions. Quill Indians who know it would doubtless have a dozen good ambush sites in mind betwixt here and where I want 'em to think we're going."

She asked, "Where *are* we going then, if not to Camp Ferris."

To which he could only reply, "Most anywhere *else,* of course. Custer might still be with us, today, had he changed directions on his way to The Place Of Greasy Grass on The Little Big Horn. We'll keep heading for Camp Ferris, dumb and anxious,'til sundown. At the pace we've been setting any fool can see we'll still be too far from town as darkness falls for anyone to be too concerned about the sounds of gunplay. They won't want to shoot it out with anyone in that tricky light betwixt dusk and starbright unless they have to. They won't think they *have* to if we hold to a steady enough pace for them to apply some rustic trigonometry to where we'll likely be coming over a rise with the Milky Way outlining our unsuspecting forms."

She made a wry face and said, "I think I'd better go back home and let someone else worry about Claudette, if only I get through the night alive. I'm not about to push on to Casper Ferry, alone, with Arapaho out acting silly, and you say you can't ride with me any farther than the next range to the northeast?"

He nodded but said, "Let's just eat this apple a bite at a time and, like you said, concentrate on making her through the coming darkness in shape to ride on *anywheres,* hear?"

By sundown Longarm had heard more about Marie and her wayward sister than the Justice Department could possibly be interested in. They kept to the same pace, in the same direction, until starbright and a tad beyond. Then Longarm called a halt in a draw, tried staring straight, then off to one side like the experienced night fighter he was, and decided, "We're both dressed dark and neither of these army bays stand out in the dark. But that white-splotched paint you're on will have to go. I can afford to discard my cheap packsaddle and we can divvy up the supplies to pack aboard our riding saddles, so . . ."

"You're going to have to shoot poor Kangi Gleska for me, then." She cut in, adding, "I've only had him a short while but I'd still feel two-hearted, killing such a trusting friend."

Longarm chuckled and replied, "So might I, and the sound might carry farther than we'd want it to. You told me, before, you picked that paint up down in Rawlins. I know the livery there you say you found near the rail depot. That pony doubtless recalls it better than either of us and any pony turned loose with no better place to head for eventually heads for the last place it was fed and watered regular."

She laughed uncertainly and said, "I like that idea better. But how am I to push on for Casper Ferry when the time comes for us to split up?"

He swung out of his McClellan to unload the other bay as he told her, "We can pick up more horseflesh off that cavalry detachment at Camp Ferris."

She told him she'd heard by tom-tom telegraph that the War Department had cut the cadre at Camp Ferris to the bone, if that, thanks to how tame things had gotten since most of the Lakota Confederacy had wound up dead or up Canada way since their big win at Little Big Horn.

He said, "I've been trying in vain to get a pay raise out of old penny pinching President Hayes since him and his Lemonade Lucy said I couldn't bring a jug into court with me no matter how tedious the case might seem. But if we can't get you a fresh pony off the remount service or one of the cow outfits springing up along the Seminoe slopes we can surely get you fixed up at Splitrock Crossing on the Sweetwater. From there you only have to follow the Sweetwater down to where it meets up with the North Platte and from there . . ."

"I knew how to get to Casper Ferry when I left Rawlins," she cut in, dismounting as well to help him reshuffle the saddles. That kept them both a mite gruntsome for casual conversation. So he didn't ask what in blue blazes she meant to do about a fifteen-year-old running wild with wandering Canadian breeds, when and if she ever caught up with 'em. He was afraid she might tell him and, as wards of the government, imperiled Indians could be of federal interest. But Billy Vail hadn't sent him north to guard the lives or even morals of the Mako Wastey sisters and renegade Arapaho were a worry for the B.I.A. if he could possibly avoid the sons of bitches.

Once they'd sent Kangi Gleska off at a confused trot with a couple of good licks from Longarm's hat-brim and left the pine packsaddle to the coming winds of winter, Longarm proceeded to avoid other company by setting a course due south. He knew he was likely on to something when even his Indian companion seemed surprised.

Marie asked, "Why are we riding *this* way? There is nothing ahead of us, nothing, before one comes to the cross country railroad tracks, at least thirty miles from here."

He chuckled and replied, "More like thirty-five. That ain't where we're headed. I mean what I said about seeing you safe at least as far north as the Sweetwater. But long before we could get there, tonight, anyone laying for us the way we've been riding all afternoon would be sure to wonder what could be taking us so long."

She said, "Pooh, not even an Absaroka could track only two ponies walking across the dried grass of autumn, after dark."

He told her he'd just said that, adding, "We're only moving an hour or so out of our way, Miss Marie. Then we'll camp high and dark, away from firewood or water, and by sunrise they ought to assume we went around 'em, either in to Camp Ferris or on to the north, as you just suggested."

She digested that in silence as they rode quietly south in the starlight for a spell. Then she asked him, in a desperately casual tone, "Are you sure you're not just out to change your luck? It's my kid sister who leaps in and out of bed with strangers, not *me*, damn it."

He laughed lightly and soothed, "I thought we'd agreed I wasn't so strange and, even if I was we got separate sleeping bags and no call for sleeping at the same time. I can generally last seventy-two hours without sleep if I need to and when your wilder kin could be after my hair I do feel the need. So I'll thank you to eat your cold pork and beans, drink your tomato preserves, and bed down alone whilst me and Mr. Winchester stand guard."

Before she could answer they heard a distant fusillade of rifle fire. As she started to rein in he muttered, "Keep going. Don't let's lope, though. Hoofbeats carry in the still night air as well and that sounded like a Spencer repeater popping less than two miles off."

27

She gasped, "Maybe closer. But who could be shooting anything at what, at this hour?"

He suggested, "I told you the white blazes on that paint glared out in the starlight, Miss Marie. After that things get less certain. Gunshots echo odd across rolling prairie. So they could have been tailing us all this time or, just as likely, an old livery nag who'd been over this prairie a time or more could have recalled oats and water, closer, at the settlement ahead. In either case, by now the rascal or rascals who just dry-gulched the poor brute should have figured out there was nobody riding it. So, like I said, let's just mosey on down to the south and put more distance betwixt ourselves and the late Kangi Gleska, hear?"

Chapter 4

Marie kept muttering to herself in her native dialect as Longarm led the way for close to a full hour with his cocked-and-fully-loaded Winchester braced across his upper thighs. The Indian girl seemed to take it as a personal insult that they'd peppered her pony with full intent to pepper *her*. Longarm agreed anyone who'd been scouting her as she'd been scouting him should have known who they'd be most likely to blow off the only black-and-white pony in the bunch. He told her not to take it so personal, explaining, "From all that rifle fire we heard back yonder they must have spotted flashes of white in the starlight and blazed away at all concerned. I'm sure the one or more blazers are more worried than we are, right now."

She poutingly asked how come. So he pointed out, "When they moved in to finish us off they found nobody there. Whether they got your paint pony total or not they sure must have wondered where you, me, and the other two went."

He reached absently for a smoke, realized how dumb that was, and continued, "How would you like to be one or more reservation jumpers blundering about in the dark with at least one armed and dangerous Wasichu onto your general whereabouts and even a skeleton force of Blue Sleeves within earshot of your fusillade-gone-wrong?"

She decided. "Heya, I think I would be riding as fast as I could for almost anwhere else, right now. But what if they are headed *this* way?"

He shrugged and said, "We'll hear 'em before they hear us, if they're riding sudden. If they're riding slow I don't see how they'll catch up with us."

The sky was so clear at this altitude that it was tempting to stand in the stirrups and see how many stars one might be able to catch in one's hat. The Milky Way shed almost as much light all around as a new moon might have. But Longarm knew a half-moon would be coming up most any time now. So when they found themselves on an unusually high swell he reined in and told her, "Like Brother Brigham was prone to say, this must be the place. We'll tether the ponies in the draw beyond and spread our bedrolls on the ungrazed crest here. Come the moonrise we'll be able to see movement from up here further than anyone moving ought to spot our stationary selves, hear?"

She said she'd camped on the High Plains in tense times before and reported chokecherry and rabbitbrush when she returned from tethering the two army bays in the inky shadows of the draw to the south.

By this time he'd spread their bedrolls in the shin-deep grass atop the rise. It was the unusually lush breed of shortgrass the Indians called "greasy." It was no such thing when one lay down in it. It just had thicker stems and more nutritious blades for grass-eating critters to thrive on. Horse Indians praised any good food by calling it fat and greasy. Greasy grass smelled more like timothy or lucerne hay to a West-By-God-Virginia boy.

Marie Mako Wastey was too assimilated to call tomato preserves or even his canned beans greasy as they shared a cold supper on the rise, each sitting cross-legged atop the bedrolls he'd spread fairly close but not too fresh. She didn't need black coffee to help her fall asleep after a long day in the saddle. Had there been a safe way to brew some he'd have surely drunk at least a quart. For at this time of the year the nights were about as long as the days and it would have been dumb even to smoke some time away atop their lookout up among the high-country stars.

30

By the time she'd polished off two whole cans he'd planned on opening in another day or more she announced she was sleepy. He didn't ask why when she wandered off in the dark a spell to brush her teeth or whatever before turning in. The secret of Victorian manners, in a world of literal horsepower and uncertain plumbing, was to never notice a carriage horse shitting almost in your face or ask a member of the opposing gender where he or she might be going as they ducked into the nearest cover.

Having been raised proper by poor but honest parents, Longarm just took advantage of the pretty Absaroka's temporary absence to stroll off the opposite way and water some soapweed on the north slope. Still young enough for strong bladder control, Longarm hadn't known how bad he'd needed to piss 'til he got to do so, long and hard with a sigh of pure pleasure.

He told the usually concealed weapon to lie back down and behave its fool self as he tucked it back in his jeans and headed back for the bedrolls, buttoning up. He hadn't quite finished when he heard the girl calling out to him, in a mighty worried tone. So he circled in from the southwest, his .44-40 drawn, to spy her and her alone standing over their bedrolls with her own six-gun drawn and waving about sort of anxious.

Knowing how a startled James Butler Hickok had once gunned a deputy coming up behind him by surprise, Longarm dropped back and to one side as he softly announced, "It's all right, Miss Marie. I ain't run off with no circus and how come you're waving that gun around?"

She hoisted her skirts knee high and bent to put her own weapon away as she declared, "I was afraid something had happened to you when I came back from, ah, petting our ponies to find myself all alone up here. I'm scared, Custis. I'm not like you about smelling Arapaho. Can you smell me, right now, by the way?"

He reholstered his own sidearm as he rejoined her, soothing, "Not as anything disgusting, if that's what you meant. I ain't dead certain I smelled that *other* Indian, earlier today. I could have just as easily *heard* something with the back of

31

my brain. Quill Indians rustle a tad different from the rest of us as well, you know."

She sank back down to her bedding but didn't get under the covers as she decided, "You're just being polite when you include me with the rest of your sweet-scented nation, right?"

He sat down nearby, saying, "Wrong. In the first place I never said my own race smelled *better* than any other. It's simply a fact of nature that different sorts of folk look, sound and, all right, smell a mite different. It's a matter of what we eat, wear and wash with more than it could be our natural juices. I never noticed it 'til a Chinee lady out Frisco way mentioned it, but you can tell when you're leaving Chinatown because they don't cook with any dairy products and most everyone else in Frisco does."

He chucked fondly; that China doll had been awfully pretty, and recalled, "I don't mind saying I felt mighty red-faced when it first occurred to me that, next to Chinee folk, the rest of us smell as if we'd spilled butter all over ourselves. The feeling passes as soon as you've been in the company of white folk for a time, of course. I doubt Mexicans notice that corn meal and peppery tang to their own parts of town unless they've been somewheres else a spell. The whole town of Denver smells as if someone's burning leaves, somewhere down the next block, the first evening you arrive. But naturally you notice other smells more, once you've been there just a few days."

She softly said, "I think I see what you mean. I can tell Indians live in a neighborhood I've never been before. Yet I can't say why and my own mother's kitchen never smelled odd to me, growing up."

He said, "Nobody's mother's kitchen ever smelled odd to 'em. How else do you think them Romans managed to swallow peacock tongues cooked in olive oil whilst Eskimo kids begged for second helpings of sea gull, well aged in decayed herrings? What you pick up in strange Indian surroundings is likely the things Indian cooks do with sugar, salt and smoke."

She said her own mother, albeit less primitive than he seemed to think, hadn't *used* much sugar or salt. So he

32

nodded and said, "That's what I meant. We've already mentioned the use of white flour instead of cream and sugar in coffee. No offense, but your folk just don't share my folk's notion of seasoning or the mixing of flavors, albeit they do say Eskimo share your taste for blackberries mushed up with unsalted lard and I'll agree smoked jerky has more flavor than air-dried, if you'll agree hickory smoke's a slight improvement over dried buffalo dung."

She laughed but said she'd do no such thing, insisting the flavor imparted by the smoke of sun-and-wind-cured shit was more delicate than anything *his* kind smoked meat with. She teased, "Do you rub the hams of a yellow-haired Wasichu woman down with sugar and salt before you find them tasty?"

He laughed and said, "Some of 'em soak their hams in violet toilet water before they offer any servings. We're likely to get along a heap better if we cut the arch remarks about each other's ancestry. I never asked to be Wasichu any more than you asked to be Absaroka, hear?"

She said she bet he was still glad he'd been born a big white man instead of a stinky little squaw.

He grimaced and said, "All right, let's forget about being friends if you want to describe yourself with a word your own nation considers insulting. Cheyenne or Arapaho gals don't mind being described by that term, by the way, since squaw just means gal in Algonquin dialects."

She cut in with, "Oh, Custis, let's not fight any more. Can't you tell the way I want you, in my own stinky savage way?"

To which he could only reply with an incredulous laugh, "I'm tired of saying you smell just as sweet as Queen Victoria, at least. I'm open to suggestions about savage feelings."

She chortled, "Wastey!" and proceeded to shuck her duds with more skill than shyness as he gulped and felt obliged to warn her, "I still got to keep riding on, once we reach the Sweetwater, Miss Marie."

She said she understood and asked why he was just sitting there with all his *own* duds on as she slipped her own plump starlit flesh under her covers, naked as a jay.

33

He knew she was more worried about the growing chill in the thin dry air than she could have been about modesty. So he got to work on his own buttons, even as he unlashed the rifle boot from his nearby McClellan to lay the Winchester handy between their bedrolls.

She coyly asked again as he slid his own naked flesh under the covers and into hers and he was only saying the simple truth when he assured her she smelled just grand. For the natural body odors of a halfways clean woman starting to get wet with desire had the most expensive French perfume beat by miles. She was so tight with passion she sort of squished as he thrust in and out of her while she panted in his face like a puppy, or lots of Indian gals, and moaned nice things to him in her own lingo—if that was what "Eh-han-key-con wi-da-ya-kah pey-lo!" meant. She couldn't have been begging him to stop if those hip movements meant anything at all.

Neither of them got much sleep that night. Longarm got none at all because he forced himself to stay awake whilst she got to doze off betwixt mad intervals of frenzied love-making. He felt no call to doubt her when she said she hadn't been getting it as regular as her wilder kid sister, but sharing a bedroll with a sister even wilder than this one was an awesome thing to contemplate.

There was more to hold an eye's interest after the moon came up to dust everything within, say, a quarter mile with silvery cigar ash. Bare tawny tits in dim moonlight were more interesting by far than the rolling sea of grass all around 'em. But Longarm still kept his eyes peeled for less friendly Indians as he admired hell out of his pleasingly plump little Absaroka.

She kept pleading with him to assure her she didn't smell too primitive and said she couldn't understand how she'd missed an unwashed savage sneaking up on the two of them.

He told her that other Indian he'd sensed more than he'd heard or sniffed had likely been closer to him than her when he'd leaped to that wrong conclusion as to who might be scouting whom that afternoon.

34

Rolling her further over on her plump breasts and belly for a deeper delving of her less-mysterious red hide, he remarked in mingled pleasure and puzzlement, "I've been known to try chess moves when the name of the game was checkers in my time. Since neither of us seem capable of describing the sneaky rascal it's entirely possible he wasn't any breed of Indian at all! I could have been thrown off my spotting this sweet Indian rump of your own in country I recalled as Indian because of that Shoshone scare a spell back. So let's go back to the beginning and figure out why *you* were scouting me whilst he, she or it was scouting the both of us."

The Absaroka girl arched her spine to take him deeper as she said, "When I spotted you by that lake I was afraid you might do *this* to me. How was I supposed to know it would feel this good? Do it faster, faster, faster! I am . . . Reyrahahhh!"

When he asked her, more face to face but just as deeply felt, she allowed she'd just said she was coming, a heap, in her own sweet way. She agreed that mysterious whatever they'd been playing some sneaky game with could have been from most any nation, since none she could come up with had any better motive to attack Indians and whites who'd never started out this friendly.

She must have gone on thinking about it whilst he circled out a ways in his birthday suit with the Winchester, sneaking another piss as well as making certain they had the whole rise to themselves. For when he returned, wind-dried and goose-bumped, to slide back in where everything was warmer, Marie said, "Hear me, I don't think Claudette and her worthless Canadian could be worth my own young life. I think it would be better if I turned back before I got hurt, chasing them all over and maybe never catching them!"

He snuggled her young lively body closer and agreed, "Now you're making sense. I never saw how you'd get your kid sister away from that older cuss without gunning him and you know how fussy the law can be about such family disputes. If the cuss is being mean to her she'll likely leave him without your help. If he ain't being mean to her, why make her leave him in the first place?"

35

Marie sighed and kissed his collarbone before asking, "Could you let me have just one tashunka to carry me south to the railroad stop at Rawlins?"

He kissed the part in her hair and replied, "Fort Steele would save you some rail fare if you mean to board an eastbound. But I got a better plan. We ain't but a few hour's ride from Camp Ferris and if you can abide that much more of my company we can pick you up *two* ponies and a day's trail supplies as well, there. That way, neither one of us will have to skimp or be slowed down by one overloaded mount, see?"

She pouted she'd lose at least half a day getting home, his way.

He chuckled fondly and said, "I was wondering how come you were so far from anywhere sensible with one pony and no coffee of your own when first we met. Being impetuous seems to run in your family. You ought to learn to look before you leap, Miss Marie. I look at railroad timetables all the time. So I can assure you you'd make the U.P. Night Flier, eastbound, easy, if we got you headed for Fort Steele my way."

She didn't answer. Some Indians could be like that, too, when they didn't seem to be getting their way. Longarm knew better than to try and josh her out of it or, worse yet, give in. He rolled on his belly and plucked a greasy grass stem to suck on in lieu of the smoke he was really dying for. After a while Marie seemed asleep, or sulking mighty serious for such a naturally warm-natured little thing.

He let her just lie there, doing either. They'd have heaps of time to kiss and make up, or not make up, betwixt where they were and where they could outfit her sensible before they split up.

He knew she'd be justified in fussing at him if he couldn't rustle her up some riding stock and trail supplies at Camp Ferris. But should the civilian settlers have pulled out along with the army they could doubtless find a cattle spread willing to do business in those same swell Seminoe foothills. The army had only occupied that strategic site, back in the seventies, because there were so many well-watered draws between gentle grazing slopes and everyone had known

36

childish Indians had no call to occupy southwest-facing timber, grass, and water that close to a handy railroad.

By the time the half moon was low to the west and the eastern sky was fading from star-spangled ebony to royal purple, Longarm was mighty relieved and suffering a mighty urge to relieve himself. So he murmured, "It'll soon be dawn and I mean to make sure nobody drops in on us unexpected for breakfast, Miss Marie. So don't you get anxious if I take a mite longer, scouting out a ways, hear?"

She didn't answer. She'd turned her brown back and broad ass to him some time before. Farther along, like the old song went, he'd find more about it. It was entirely possible she just liked to sleep on that side. She-male tactics were sure confusing, as they were doubtless meant to be.

As he crawled back out it felt colder than a banker's heart and his first impulse was to haul on some duds. But there seemed no call to haul pants on and off so much for no more than sissy reasons. So he strode south through the lightly frosted grass on his bare feet with just the Winchester to find the two army bays calmly steaming in the even colder predawn stillness of the draw where Marie had secured them to chokecherry trunks. One of the ponies nickered at him when he quietly called out, "I'll be back around sunrise with your breakfast oats and bag-water, boys."

They were in no position to argue. It would have been rude to squat and drop it on that side of the rise, knowing neither ponies nor Indian ladies were likely to enjoy the aroma of his morning crap. So he followed the contour line of the slope around to the west, where, with nobody but that low half-moon for company, he could hunker down in the grass, bracing himself with the butt of his saddle gun, and get rid of all those canned beans and tomato preserves he'd been eating of late. Canned pork and beans sure got pungent on its way through a cuss. He was glad no morning breezes seemed to be blowing upslope from the west.

Wiping himself well with clumps of sun-cured shortgrass, Longarm rose to continue his patrol, a quarter mile or more out from their discreet campsite on the summit. A couple of horned larks he'd disturbed cussed

him out and there were always less identifiable critters skittering ahead of one through the grass in the
dark. But it seemed safe to say that mysterious rider
they'd been worried about had ridden on to scare someone else.

He felt chilled to the bone by the time he got back to
the bedrolls. So he shoved the Winchester back in its boot
and slid his frozen hide back in Marie's warm bedroll as he
chortled, "Kee-rist this feels fine and if my balls ain't froze
all the way through I'll . . . What the hell?"

Marie wasn't there. He started to call out to her. Then he
nodded sagely and decided, "Right, Queen Victoria likely
shits at least once a year but you'd never know it, to watch
her in public."

So he snuggled down deeper amid her Hudson Bay blankets, feeling warmer already and inspired by that violet
toilet water you could just make out with your head under
the covers.

Hudson Bay was both a style and brand of blankets, with
both red and white customers so attached to the name and
rep that unethical New England mills had been known
to weave imitations of the superior British product. The
Hudson Bay fur-trading monopoly had sins of its own to
answer for, according to John Jacob Astor and many another rival from south of the Canadian border, but cheating
trappers and hunters with shoddy trade goods wasn't one
of them. The soft thick blankets Hudson Bay swapped for
prime pelts, with the weight of the blanket and number of
pelts it was worth indicated by woven-in black stripes, were
traded far and wide among others who'd never been near
a Hudson Bay trading post. Longarm idly decided to ask
Marie, when she got back, whether her own trading daddy
bought direct from the Canadian outfit. Hudson Bay would
sell its goods by mail order and the blankets in this bedroll
seemed too new to have been swapped back and forth all
that much.

After he'd waited a spell longer he began to worry more
about Marie than about her bedding. She'd been out there,
bare-ass, longer than he had, and he'd been ball-puckered
good by the time he'd gotten back under these covers.

38

He propped himself up on one bare elbow to gaze about for some sign of a naked lady in the now-gray dawn. He saw his own duds spread across the frosted grass to one side. He didn't see her boots, hat or newer denim duds. She'd as obviously taken her gun along. There was nothing in the U.S. Constitution saying a lady couldn't get dressed and pack a gun when she went to take a morning crap. But as long as they were paying him to have a suspicious nature Longarm felt obliged to crawl back out, haul on his own boots, duds and six-gun, and pick up that Winchester again to go see what there might be to see.

It didn't take him long to see she'd lit out with one of the army bays he'd told he she couldn't have. He wasn't certain until he got back to the top of the rise that she'd slipped away in the predawn darkness with her own saddle, a few cans of grub, and a sack of oats for the pony she'd made up her stubborn mind to steal.

Longarm sighed and murmured aloud, "Perfidy, thy name is Woman and Damn Fool, thy name is *Me*, as usual. When are you ever going to learn *they* can lie whilst coming just as good as *we* can?"

He knew he could likely catch up with her, if he started right now, just as she'd known, starting out, why he wasn't likely to ride after her. Billy Vail hadn't sent him out after Indian horse thieves and, even if he caught that particular one he was likely to look dumb as hell in court when she demurely insisted she'd swapped him valuable trade goods and other favors for just one teeny-weeny little gelding.

So he said, "Fuck it." Then he brightened and added, "Come to study on it, I just did and I can always pick up another pack brute in that settlement ahead. So who's to say who came out ahead this cold gray dawn?"

Chapter 5

The rolling range got less open as it rolled higher to the northeast. He kept an eye peeled for that paint they'd abandoned to the luck of the draw. But he had a tough enough time spotting the chimney smoke of Camp Ferris above a considerable patch of second-growth aspen with all those hazy Seminoes beyond the dinky trail break.

Little more than a general store cum post office and a combined wheelwright and smithy had stayed behind to serve the local nesters and stockmen, mostly stockmen, once the army had pulled out.

Nobody there seemed to care. They said they hadn't heard tell of any Indian trouble that summer or fall and seemed surprised to learn he'd seen even a tame one within a day's ride. The blacksmith fixed him up with another pony, this one a cordovan mare, and they were naturally proud to sell him another cheap packsaddle and some mighty expensive canned goods to make up for what that pretty but hungry Absaroka gal had either eaten or stolen from him. He felt no call to tell on her in Camp Ferris. Had there been a telegraph left he might have wired the Crow Agency she was still alive and likely on her way home. Since the army had pulled down the wire whilst pulling up stakes there was no way he could. So he paid up, shook friendly all around, and rode on just after a noon sit-down of soup and soda crackers with the nice old couple who ran the general store. He knew it wasn't their fault they had to charge so much for goods packed in so far by mule train. They'd given him a fair price on the hand-hewn packsaddle of local lodgepole pine and refused to take anything for the second helping of soup and crackers.

The rest of his day, spent riding solo through modest patches of timber and vaster stretches of shortgrass, would have been even more tedious if he hadn't been concerned about possible enemies and an almost certain change for the worse in the weather ahead.

Reining in a pair of dark brown ponies in tall timber to dismount and pussyfoot back for a spell of brooding over one's backtrail made it seem unlikely anyone was trailing him, once he'd done that more than half a dozen times at staggered intervals. So unless the sneak who'd been scouting him, Marie, or both was trailing Marie the other way, it seemed likely they'd thrown him off in the dark the night before. He surely hadn't ridden into Camp Ferris, and the folk there had said they hadn't paid mind to any distant shots they might or might not have heard just after sundown. But as he'd assured Marie just after they'd heard 'em closer, nobody making all that noise that close to any settlement could be certain he'd be safe to hang about indefinitely.

Telling himself the rascal could have been a loco loner of either the white or red persuasion and hence not worth deep study until such time as he did something spooky again, Longarm decided to worry more about the wild Wyoming sky up yonder. There was hardly any wind down here at saddle level. Yet the various ominous shades of gray that had hidden the sun entirely were commencing to churn in all sorts of swirling patterns as if he was staring up from the depths of God's washbasin on a long delayed laundry day, and only God knew what he was fixing to dump in for one bodacious scrubbing.

So when he spied more wood smoke streaming sideways through taller lodgepoles to his right Longarm headed that way, even though it was out of his way to the Split Rock crossing of the Sweetwater to his northwest. For there was just no way he was going to make Split Rock, a good two

41

dozen miles from Camp Ferris, before it rained fire and salt to flood every draw and then some.

An unseen pony nickered at his strange mounts from the thick timber ahead. So he drew his .44-40 and pegged a couple of friendly shots at the swirling thunderheads above, lest someone get the notion he was trying to ease in on 'em without an invite.

He knew his shots had been heard when, just before he rode into the pine boughs almost meeting to either side, he heard someone calling out, "That's far enough, Mister. This here's private property and as you must have noticed by now there's miles and miles of nothing but miles and miles you'd be safer trespassing across, hear?"

Longarm reined in but called back, "I ain't a mister, I'm the law, federal, and I ain't as anxious to trespass as I am to get in out of the rain."

"It ain't raining," the surly voice called back.

To which Longarm dryly replied, "I can see you're a stranger to this high country if you can't feel rain and taste lightning once it gets this close. I'll ride on and take my chances with the coming storm if you got something back in all them pines you just don't want the law to know about. I'm a deputy marshal, not a revenue rider, if that's any help."

There was a long pause, punctuated by a distant roll of thunder. Then the unseen surly cuss decided, "Come on in, then. Makes more sense to coffee and cake an unwelcome pest than it does to get raided by a whole posse for no good reason in the sweet by and by."

Longarm agreed that was about the size of it and dismounted with his reloaded six-gun politely holstered lest anyone suspect him of sinister intent, or try any sinister intentions on an unwary rider with all sorts of tree branches whipping at his fool face.

Leading his bay gelding and cordovan mare with both reins and trail line gripped casually in his left hand, Longarm penetrated the gloom to meet up with a cat-eyed young cuss dressed cow and armed serious for even a wary nester. The double-barreled ten gauge he had cradled over one forearm would have been enough to greet unexpected visitors with.

42

The Schofield .45 on each hip indicated mighty valuable property worth guarding, or taking, as soon as one considered how cheap the rest of his outfit looked.

The kid was blue-eyed but tan as some purebloods Longarm had met up with in his time. He said his handle was Lamont, Scotty Lamont, but didn't offer to shake as he added, "Might as well get on back to the cabin for that coffee and cake, like I said. But Aunt Flora ain't going to like this."

As he followed the heavily armed but ragged-ass youth through the tanglewood Longarm nodded thoughtfully and observed, "I've heard of your clan, Scotty. I can't say how big it was back in Scotland but they do say there's a heap of you Lamonts up in this part of Wyoming Territory."

The still far-from-friendly kid muttered, "You're learning. We got our own town named after us, not far from here, and nobody messes with us no matter *where* they meet up with us in this basin, hear?"

Before Longarm had to locate the trail town of Lamont in his mental map they were out of the pines and he could see the low-slung ramble of sod-roofed log structures and corral rails filling most of the clearing ahead. A natural spring drained by a plank-lined brook they had to step over explained most everything else. A well-watered glade sheltered from winter winds by evergreen timber would be worth more than it looked to any stock outfit, come the first blizzards any time now and the spring thaw Lord only knew when.

The ferociously armed kid told him he could run his ponies in with the others whilst he in turn prepared his Aunt Flora for uninvited guests.

Longarm unsaddled both brutes in the main corral but left them bridled and tethered under a shingled overhang above the water troughs at the north end. The other half dozen head he was leaving his own stock with would likely be sensible once it commenced to storm out here. But strange stock penned in strange surroundings tended to tear around in dangerous circles, seeking the comforts of the more familiar they just couldn't get at.

One of the ponies who felt more at home there came over to see if the cordovan mare wanted to screw. Longarm left them to work that out as he headed for what seemed the kitchen door of the main house with both his pack and riding saddle balanced on his left shoulder.

A somewhat older, hawk-faced individual appeared in the doorway as he approached, calling out, "Leave 'em out here by the washstand. Scotty said you was the law?"

Longarm replied, "Your pard's right about that. You're wrong about me leaving gear exposed to the elements when the Wyoming sky turns elemental as *that!* You sure you ride this range regular, old son?"

The new face smiled thinly and replied, "Scotty's the old boy born out this way. I come up from Texas this spring. Name's Winchel. They call me Waco more often, though."

Longarm said he'd remember that as he followed the hatchet-faced one inside, load and all. When he saw the little old sparrow dressed in black widow's weeds and a sort of cobweb shawl staring beady-eyed at him from the far side of the cast-iron range he quickly deposited both saddles on the floor, just inside the screen door, to remove his hat entire and say, "I had to, Ma'am. It's fixing to really rain outside. While I could likely manage aboard a damp McClellan for a few days I ain't sure about how waterproof my packs might be."

The one calling himself Scotty Lamont stepped through the doorway behind the old woman to say, "Aunt Flora ain't sore, Mister. She's just not used to talking English. All the elders in our family come out here talking Scotch Gaelic. But set yourself yonder and I'll ask her to rustle us up some refreshings."

Longarm nodded soberly at the tense looking Aunt Flora and hung his hat on a peg driven into the log-chinking as he eased around to the far side of her unpainted pine table. But he remained on his feet with his back to a kitchen corner as the one called Scotty proceeded to order Aunt Flora about in what might have passed for the Gaelic to a man who'd spent less time in the American West.

Waco, lounging against the jamb of the back door, told Longarm to go ahead and set. Longarm said he'd been brought up to wait on the lady of the house taking her own seat at the table. Waco wore his Patterson Conversion low in a tie-down cutaway. Scotty was more interesting to contemplate as he stood in that opposite doorway with that ten-gauge held polite but doubtless fully charged with number nine buck.

Aunt Flora moved just out of Longarm's line of fire to open a perforated tin pie safe against the wall to his left. He knew it could still be a tight fight if he just slapped leather. He still felt duty-bound to announce, "All right, everybody freeze and if I'm wrong I'll sure be first to apologize."

Nobody did. Aunt Flora dropped to the floor to roll under the table as the muzzles of that ten gauge rose like a nineteen-year-old dick in Dodge on payday. So Longarm drew and fired on Scotty first.

Both barrels of the two-faced rascal's ten-gauge blasted into the flooring between them as Longarm's pistol round slammed through his breastbone. Then the hatchet-faced Waco was trying to draw and crawfish out the back door at the same time. So Longarm nailed him less neatly, but neatly enough, with only half his lower jaw torn away.

Longarm waded through the swirling haze of gunsmoke to finish that one with a more merciful round in the chest. As he turned back to call out to the old woman he could just make her out, back on her feet in all that gunsmoke, clicking the hammers of the empty shotgun she had trained on him.

He said, "Not *me,* Ma'am. *Them.* I got 'em both and how long have they had you and this spread at their mercy?"

She dropped the ten-gauge on the table between them with a happy sob and wailed in plain rural American, "Since just before sunrise and you were an even better lawman than they feared! They told me we'd both die on the spot if I said one word to you, just now! How did you ever read my mind like that?"

He reloaded his warm six-gun as he modestly explained, "I couldn't tell why you were so on edge and I speak the Gaelic about as well as I play Scotch bagpipes. But I'd heard *Chinook* before and since it's a baby-talk Indian trade

45

jargon I was even able to follow the kid's drift."

The smoke had cleared enough by now for both of them to make out Scotty's spurred boots in that inner doorway as Longarm soberly went on, "He wasn't telling you anything, Ma'am. He'd already said in pure English what he wanted you to do next. So as you proceeded to do so, he was suggesting to his pard it might be best to hear me out before they both gunned me, under the table, with my fool elbows up on top."

She looked as if she was trying not to scream. He nodded and said, "I'd have likely been more alert than that. Well before Scotty as much as confessed they were owlhoot riders I'd been wondering a mite about 'em. To begin with it's unusual to have ponies instead of yard dogs barking at strangers in such out of the way country, no offense."

She sobbed, "They shot our old redbone, Gilliedubh, as they rode in. Then they were upon me before I could get yon shotgun my late husband, Tavish, knew how to use better than me!"

Longarm soothed, "I'm sure you'd have stopped 'em coming across your doorstep, judging by how well you point it, if only you'd had time to load it. But all's well as ends well and the only question before the house, now, is exactly how we want to end this. You say they found you and all them ponies out back alone and unguarded on such an out-of-the-way spread, no offense?"

She shook her gray head to reply, "Oh, I'd never manage out here all by myself. My daughter and her husband, Bruce, are usually here with me, along with our two tame Utes, Freddy and Jack. The kids and our hands drove a remuda of half-broke ponies up to the Wind River Country to help stock one of those new beef operations east of Fort Washakie."

Longarm nodded but said, "I'd still best carry you on in to the safer surroundings of Split Rock, Ma'am. I ain't sure either of us would enjoy that long a ride in the company of dead men in high summer but it's already cooling off outside and do we chill 'em well overnight and get an early start with both of 'em well wrapped in wet canvas . . ."

"I can't leave this property and all our stock unguarded!" She cut in, adding, "It's fixing to rain any minute. It may be raining well into the morrow and if only you could stay until the others get back . . ."

He shook his head soberly and replied, "I can't, Ma'am. I'm already running a tad late, and if I don't get to a telegraph and wire in a position report soon, my boss is apt to have the pesky U.S. Cav out looking for me."

There came a distant rumble from the darkening sky outside, as if Wakan Tonka was trying to tell him something. He nodded and said, "I'd be dumb to ride on, with or without you, before sunrise, wet or dry. Meanwhile I'd best hang this dead meat up to cool before they mess your flooring more or the rats come out to mess with either of 'em."

The hawk-faced Waco lay handier to the outside. So Longarm hunkered down to deal first with that one as Aunt Flora sniffed and protested she allowed no rats about the house.

He didn't argue. It might have been *mice* he could smell, away from the embers of her kitchen range. He found nothing on Waco more valuable than his gun rig and a pigskin wallet holding forty-six dollars and not a penny's worth of identification.

Hauling that cadaver just outside, Longarm moved in to treat the remains of the so-called Scotty Lamont the same way, with about the same results, before he began to drag the dead boy out back by his booted ankles, observing, "Even strangers like me have heard tell of all the Scotch Sinclairs, Lamonts and such that come to settle these parts after the buffalo and Indians had been thinned to reasonable proportions. They must have known your name before they promoted you to this one's aunt. The other one was a dumber fibber. He said he hailed from Texas under a hat telescoped in the north range fashion. Then he said this one had been *born and raised* up here, on range that was pure Quill Indian when I was scouting Shoshone for the army just a few short summers back!"

She told him she'd been a widow woman with a married daughter at the time and said she'd fix them both some supper whilst he hauled the bodies over to the smoke house. She said he'd find that just downwind of the back bunkhouse but upwind of the stables and corrals.

He wasn't surprised. That was about where anyone with a lick of delicacy would want to smoke their meat. It took him two trips, of course, and whilst the interior of the small, stuffy smoke house held two and a half sides of blackened beef, the hardwood coals in the central fire pit were dead as a whore's eyes.

He found two unoccupied meat hooks and wrestled both cadavers into awkward upright positions. He hooked both through the collars of their stout work shirts instead of their clammy flesh. For would *you* hang future table meat on rusty steel you'd sunk in a cuss who could have been most anywhere since his last decent bath?

Aunt Flora fried a fair mess of onions, steak and spuds to go with their Scotch coffee. You made Scotch coffee instead of Irish coffee by leaving out the cream and stirring in more whiskey. As they sat across from one another in warm comfort whilst the thunderbird flapped ever closer out in the dark, she said she'd heard about that other old widow running for Sheriff a county or so to the north. But she failed to see what all the fuss was about and wanted to talk more about the adventures he'd had, getting this far.

He told her, leaving out some of the dirty parts about that sweet young thing off the Crow Agency, and she seemed surer than him about Indians pestering the two of them being party to the same dark mystery.

He declined thirds helpings but accepted more liquor-laced coffee as he pointed out, "There's no saying for certain anyone but that one Absaroka gal was all that Indian. We never got a close look at the cuss scouting us, way to the south. Chinook is a made-up lingo based on at least two Indian dialects along with simple French and English. It was whipped up, way back when, to facilitate swapping for furs, women and ponies, in about that order. You don't have to be pure Indian to talk Chinook, any more than you have to be Chinee to talk tea trade pidgin."

She said both those young scamps had looked Indian to her, citing the Ute hands who were usually about as evidence of her eye for such matters.

He fished out an after-supper smoke, held the cheroot up for her to nod or frown at and, as she nodded, said, "They could have been breeds, Ma'am. That old melting pot's been stirred a heap out our way and betwixt Colonel William Bent and his two Cheyenne wives the results have confused a heap of folk. At least two of the Bent brothers fought at Sand Creek, on opposite sides, and they got a kid sister who'd look white enough to pass if she wasn't wed to a French Canadian Metís and inclined to dress up so beaded and fringed."

He thumbnailed a match head alight and got his cheroot going good before he explained, "It don't hardly matter whether them two in the smoke house were breeds living white or white horse thieves who'd had lots of dealing with red horse thieves in their time. All that really matters is that I showed up before they could finish up, here."

She stared owl eyed across the remains of their meal at him as she asked, "Oh, Lord, you may well have saved me from a fate worse than death, young man!"

He shrugged modestly and replied, "I ain't all that young and my friends call me Custis, Miss Flora."

It might have seemed heartless to add she had to be a whole heap older and that many an old gal had preferred all sorts of fates to death, once things had narrowed down to that choice. So he continued, "Be that as it may, they must have scouted this place good, knowing your name and the fact they'd find you alone out here with all them fine ponies pent out back."

"Good heavens! Do you really think they were out to steal our prize breeding stock?" she almost wailed.

To which he soothingly but convincingly replied, "That and anything else they didn't find nailed down, Miss Flora. I don't see how they could have hoped to hang on to this land and the improvements you and your kin have erected on the same. Let's say they'd heard your daughter, her man, and a couple of young Indian hands were off somewhere with other stock. What if they'd shown up

49

somewhere else with even better ponies, claiming to be those Ute hands everyone knows you-all had working out here for you?"

She shook her gray head and said, "That's silly. Freddy Antlers Shedding and Jack Surrounded look nothing like those two you just now saved me from!"

He just took a knowing drag on his cheroot. She proved him right when she blinked and added, "Oh, dear, I suppose to someone a hard day's ride from here a swarthy lad who calls himself an Indian would look much like any other he or she might have only heard about."

He said that seemed about the size of it as, outside, it was suddenly coming down in wind-whipped sheets.

She marveled, "Won't you listen to that autumn gale? Even if it lets up by morning the trails will be impassable until late afternoon, if then."

He quietly observed he'd ridden this range in the past and figured they could make the twenty-odd miles to Split Rock before the sun ever set again.

She said she wasn't about to ride all the way to Split Rock, but that she was ready to bed down for the night if he was.

He allowed it was a tad earlier than he generally went to bed. But when she asked what else he had in mind with the wind and rain howling fit to bust and not even a Monkey Ward catalogue to read by draft-flickered candlelight he had to agree he'd spent a long hard day in the saddle and that an early lie-down couldn't kill him.

He nudged his nearby McClellan with a booted toe as he offered to spread his own bedding in her hayloft or most anywhere but that smoke house.

She asked how come and said she'd feel ever so much safer locked behind the same door or more with such a strong and brave young man.

It sounded innocent enough, he decided, as he regarded her small fussy outline by the tricky light while she bustled things up off the table. When he rose to offer her a hand she told him housework was woman's work. But when he suggested putting all their supperware in a wash basin and leaving it out on the back steps for the thunderbird to lick clean she laughed like hell and favored him with a far-from-motherly kiss.

Then she stammered that she didn't know what had come over her just now and asked whatever he might think of such a dirty old lady.

He didn't tell her. He was bound and determined to carry her on in to Split Rock with him, along with those dead outlaws, come even a cold gray dawn, and he knew he'd feel just about as silly throwing and hog-tying a little old lady as he would doing anything else to her.

He was still hoping to keep it clean, even after she'd led him by the hand through the dark and drafty main house to a perfumed log chamber mostly occupied by a big four poster. When he observed she surely had a fancy bedroom she confided, shutting and bolting the the stout door with a girlish giggle, "As as matter of fact this is where my Elsbet and her man bed down, when they're here. But as you can see, they're not here, and I fear my wee trundle on the other side of the house would never hold the two of us, even if we both tried the middle, if you know what I mean."

He knew what she meant. He still felt silly as hell stripping down to his long johns, even in the dark, in the company of such a little gray-headed sparrow.

He couldn't see exactly what she might be doing on the far side of the big four poster. He assumed she'd get in from that side in her own underthings and sheepishly chided himself for wondering about that. He figured old ladies were likely innocent as little gals about such matters, neither having the equipment to feel really lusty.

As he eased gingerly between the sheets on his side he tried to recall how he'd felt about young gals and old ladies back before his own equipment had started acting so silly around womankind. Life had sure felt less complicated, back home in West-By-God-Virginia when a mess of barefoot boys and girls could watch a pair of goats going at it and idly speculate on why both critters seemed so het up.

Then old Flora had slid her bare old ass across the bottom sheet to crowd him on his side and neither she nor her ass felt all that old as she rolled half atop him, moaning like a lovesick owl-bird as he automatically took her in his arms,

51

muttering, "Well, Boss, the Good Lord can assure you this was never *my* fool notion!"

"What's wrong? Do you find me too disgusting?" the now invisible and far from shapeless woman in his arms was pleading as she popped a button tugging at the fly of his long johns, sobbing something about it having been so long, before she suddenly gasped, "Oh, Dear Lord, I didn't expect it to be *this* long!"

So he rolled her over on her bare back to run what she so admired up inside her as she hugged him tightly with her tiny arms and legs, hissing, "Yesss! Do it, Custis. Make me feel young and alive again as you come in this pitiful shell of what I once was!"

He soothed, "Aw, you ain't so pitiful, Miss Flora," as he considered but rejected that notorious essay by Ben Franklin on older women.

He wasn't sure Ben Franklin had really wrote that dirty and even if he had, he'd been sort of smug about the poor old dears. Yet it did seem true that as trees withered from the top down a healthy woman as old as this one could still have plenty of juice in her roots. For neither her belly nor bare tits felt all that withered, come to study on them in the dark. So, seeing how silly he was likely to feel in the morning in any case, he just proceeded to treat her like any other hot and hornsome she-male and, from the way she was bumping and grinding to meet every thrust, she must have felt he was treating her right.

Chapter 6

The storm had blown over before midnight, as could be the custom at that time of the year at that altitude. So the dirty old lady celebrated the sudden silence with another crime against nature, according to the moral code of Wyoming Territory, and waited 'til they'd come that way before she asked if he'd respect her in the morning.

Longarm assured her he'd always respect her at least as much as he did right now and proved it with some less complicated dog-styling. But in God's truth he felt sort of silly in the cold gray light of dawn, being served ham and eggs by a stark naked lady who was gray all over, even though he'd been right about those curves the cruel teeth of Time hadn't chewed as much.

It felt even sillier to ride better than twenty miles with two dead owlhooters and a sweet little old lady who kept calling you her Huggy Thumper and suggesting every wooded draw you led her through would make a swell spot for more thumping.

He got her to keep going by suggesting there might be a wayside inn as well as an undertaker in Split Rock, where the post road they were looking for forded the Sweetwater. He'd wrapped both bodies in cool wet canvas before lashing them face down across the ponies old Flora said they'd ridden in on. He still wanted them photographed, embalmed good, and planted shallow as soon as possible.

Checking into any sort of hired digs with a lady at least twice his age, in a small town, was a bridge he wouldn't have to cross for half a day's ride and she did look somehow younger, riding sidesaddle in a trimly tailored whipcord habit she said she was borrowing from her daughter for the occasion. He'd let her strap the two-gun rig of the younger outlaw around her surprisingly trim hips, lest they run into more outlaws or, heaven forefend, Indians. That might have helped the illusion she'd cinched her waistline with a corset, even though he knew for a fact she had nothing at all on under that buckskin-colored whipcord.

Her perky black derby was veiled and a heap of her gray hair was bunned up inside it. Longarm still felt his ears burning as they rode into the river crossing just after one in the afternoon. For you'd think they'd never seen four riders coming in before, one she-male and two face-down across their saddles.

Split Rock was nowhere near the county seat, but one of the older gents who'd come out of the barber shop half-shaved to take part in all that staring turned out to be Undersheriff Ian Huston, who rode herd on the law along the Sweetwater when he wasn't busy with his cows. They were Cherokee Longhorn, a mixture of Spanish and Durham stock, and he wanted to talk about them and the rising beef prices back east instead of a couple of saddle tramps who'd died by misadventure in another danged county entire.

The older lawman was polite enough to order two of his own deputies to lead the canvas-wrapped cadavers over to Doc Fowler's and have the undertaker-cum-deputy-coroner do something with 'em before they stunk up the town. But even as he pointed to his frame-office-cum-lock-up across the one street he insisted they'd come to the wrong law.

As Longarm helped old Flora down from her sidesaddle he told the older lawman, "I know the sheriff way down in Rawlins would have the jurisdiction if all or even most of the charges were local. But even had I wanted to backtrack to Rawlins, and even if this lady here would have been willing to accompany me that far, I'd still have a *federal* case here. I'm only asking you and your boys for an assist

54

you'll get written credit for, once I wire my home office for further instructions."

As the undersheriff helped Longarm tether the two remaining ponies to the lodgepole hitching rail in front of his jail Longarm continued, "It's my fond hope the U.S. Marshal in Cheyenne will want to send his own team here to tidy up, albeit I'd as soon investigate conspiracy, and likely murder, as voter registration."

Undersheriff Huston chuckled and opened the unlocked door for them as he said he'd heard about that doubtless plucky but surely foolish she-sheriff running for a second term up by the Shoshone Agency. The cluttered office he led them into seemed dark enough to make gray-headed ladies look girlish, a trick not accomplished by the afternoon glare outside. Huston waved old Flora to the swivel chair by a rolltop desk and hauled a bentwood visiting chair from a corner for Longarm as he said, not unkindly, "I've rid for the law federal in my day, no offense, and I'm still having a tough time following your line of reasoning, old son. Why don't you commence at the beginning and see if I can't convince you of the error of your ways?"

Longarm refused the seat with a polite shake of his head. So the older man sat down closer to the old lady, muttering he was no fool. She dimpled at him and said, "Custis is ever so smart. You should have been there when those two scamps tried to flimflam him!"

Huston observed he hadn't been. So Longarm began to tersely bring him up to date, beginning with no dogs barking where you'd think they'd keep at least one good barker. The older lawman, a Wyoming stockman as well, kept nodding but looking ever more puzzled until Longarm got as far as the shoot-out in the close quarters of that kitchen, at which point he shook his head firmly and said, "County, county and more county, Uncle Sam! As a paid-up peace officer you had the right to arrest a crime in progress and I'll allow them two you brung in must have had something mighty criminal in mind, but all of it *local* 'til you stuck your nose and your federal badge into their business."

Before Longarm could answer his elder gushed on, "You say you sort of stumbled into some conspiracy and I'll allow they must have been out to rob this dear lady or worse, but . . ."

"I said conspiracy for sure and murder most foul more than likely," Longarm cut in, smiling down dryly as he proceeded to count on his own fingers. "To begin with, none of this high country has been settled long enough for a single homestead claim to have been proven and titled fee simple, right?"

The part-time lawman and full-time stockman nodded with a frown to agree, "Everybody knows that, old son. To gain full title under the Homestead Act of '63 you got to occupy and improve the land a full five years after filing and . . . Oh, I follow your drift. But ain't you stretching it a mite to charge that jumping an unproven claim on federal land could constitute a federal crime?"

Longarm shrugged and replied, "At least it's a charge, worth the time of a federal grand jury. The details of the conspiracy are less important than murder in the first, federal. Two of the likely victims were members of a friendly Indian nation, making 'em wards of the U.S. Government and . . . No, *don't!*"

But it was already too late, and Longarm could only watch in horror as the old woman drew both of those cavalry Schofield .45's, to aim both, unfriendly, at point-blank range.

Then she and the swivel chair were going over backwards as the old undersheriff blazed away with his own Smith & Wesson no matter how hard Longarm yelled at him to stop.

By the time he'd emptied his six-gun into her, Undersheriff Huston was standing over the thoroughly shot-up woman betwixt their overturned chairs. Longarm swore softly and moved to bar the door to the street as he heard loud shouts and the sounds of running footsteps.

"She tried to kill us! Both of us! And I still can't see *why!*" The older man sobbed, staring down through the swirling gunsmoke at the motherly-looking whatever he'd just pumped full of hot lead.

Knowing they didn't have much time, Longarm got right to the point with, "I asked you not to because I'd already replaced the brass in Scotty's guns with spent rounds. I figured I ought to because even though I couldn't be sure,'til just now, I had plenty of reasons to suspect they hadn't been showing me the whole picture."

He reached absently for a cheroot, decided this might be a dumb time to light up, and explained, "You just saw how fast she could think in a tight spot. She tried to blast me with an empty ten-gauge right after I'd dropped her confederates. Then she saw I seemed to have her down as the widow Lamont they'd told me she was and decided to keep it friendly."

Huston sighed and said, "She sure smiled friendly at me,'til just before she tried to blow my fool face off with spent rounds. Get to the part about you switching brass on her, old son."

Longarm sighed and said, "Oh, I did that right off, before we, ah, turned in for the night. Ain't Huston a Scotch name, too, and, no offense, don't I detect just a hint of that heather bush in your voice when you get excited?"

Huston scowled up at him to insist, "I'm American as you are and what if my mother *was* born in Portree? She left when she was no more than six, dang it."

Longarm soothed, "I only said a *hint* of heather. That lady at our feet had none at all, on a spread where even the yard dog had a Gaelic name. After that I'd met her wearing ill-fitting widow's weeds and yet, as you can see, that riding habit fits her as if it was made for her, which it likely was. She said it was her daughter's. Lots of mothers and daughters are built about the the same. But would your average daughter ride on business to a distant town in less than her best riding outfit?"

"The gal might have had two such outfits," said Huston cautiously.

Longarm nodded and said, "I just told you I wasn't certain. It was a matter of a false note here and a lady with horsewoman's hips and no riding habit of her own there. You'd have met her in handcuffs had I been *dead* certain, but try her this way. Say a roving band of serious horse thieves had learned of a remote spread where only three men and a young woman were raising and guarding prime cow ponies."

Huston nodded soberly and said, "With the price of beef rising and this range getting more settled by the day I might be in the market for such stock, myself. But, saying they moved in on the real Lamonts down yonder, why would they want to pass this one off as their old Aunt Flora?"

Longarm shrugged and said, "They had to call her something 'til they could get rid of me one way or the other. They couldn't have passed her off as the younger lady of the house they'd doubtless disposed of long before I rode in. There might have really *been* a nice old lady living out there with her kin and them two Indian hands, in which case the team from Cheyenne should unearth five bodies. Six, counting that poor dog."

Undersheriff Huston whistled softly down at the sweet old thing he'd shot five times and marveled, "If you're right I likely shot it out with the brains of the outfit just now! It'd take brass balls as well as brains to simply move in on a stud spread and pretend to be the folk belonging there 'til you . . . what? They couldn't have hoped to get away with it forever."

Longarm shook his head and said, "I think she told me what she and her boys planned to do when she allowed the real owners and their hands had headed for more distant parts with the cream of the stock. I just stumbled over 'em as they were getting set to do so, this side of that storm we all felt coming."

"I'm starting to see how they might have hoped to get away with it," the older lawman decided, adding, "I still say, knowing names and other details in advance, it still would have called for balls of the boldest brass and . . . say, you don't suppose . . ."

"She was really a woman." Longarm cut in with a sigh. Then he caught himself about to catch himself and quickly added, "Of course, it won't hurt to have your deputy coroner check that out for us as well. For now that you mention it, she surely did act bold for what she looked like, most of the time."

• • •

Split Rock wasn't big enough to rate a regular Western Union office, but you could patch in to the old military line from the post office if you knew how. The local postmaster didn't. But he said Longarm could give her a try if he was willing to pay for fresh battery acid. The same old geezer ran the hardware and feed store. So he had some jugs of the same he'd thought he'd *never* unload before they all dried up.

Once they had telegraph connections to the outside world up to Fort Washakie by way of an interested signal corps officer, and after a weary go-ahead from Western Union's Cheyenne office, it only took Longarm a couple of hours to establish that there had indeed been a family called Lamont and a pair of Ute hands working that particular homestead claim as a stud spread, according to files at Land Management and Indian Affairs.

After that things got less certain. Any number of common-looking criminals—red, white or in between—might have picked up some Chinook jargon during mispent wanderings. The only really bad Indian the B.I.A. had out this way dressed and acting so Wasichu was an assimilated but sort of vicious Osage who failed to fit the descriptions of either old boy Longarm had met at the Lamont spread. Osage didn't talk at all like Chinook, anyway. Longarm still wired back he'd keep an eye open for their Jerry Black Wolf, wanted for robbing his council funds and more than one killing.

They had better luck asking about for anything anyone might have on really dirty old ladies answering to the description of the one on ice in Doc Fowler's cellar. Neither Longarm nor the older gents with him were surprised to learn her real name hadn't been Flora Lamont. She'd used half a dozen others in her own recent travels, but Portia Slade of Davenport, Iowa, was what they'd put on that murder warrant involving a third or fourth husband who'd been an important dealer in horseflesh before she'd shot him in front of witnesses.

Since then, under many another name, she'd surfaced here, there and yonder as a horse trader whose bills of sale

59

left a lot to be desired on closer examination.

Undersheriff Huston said he was glad he'd gunned a murderess instead of someone's dear old granny. But he said he still felt awesomely awkward about shooting any damn sort of woman.

Longarm said *he* felt awkward as well. When the older lawman asked, "How come? You didn't pump five rounds in her, did you?" Longarm had a time meeting Huston's eyes as he replied, in as innocent a tone as he could manage, "It ain't considered professional to pump anything into a suspect if it can be avoided. I was hoping to keep things friendly as possible 'til I determined how suspicious we ought to be of a lady who told possible but barely possible stories."

It seemed more logical to smoke, now that he'd about run out of others to telegraph. But he held out for fresher air to light up in as he pushed back from the desk set, saying, "At least I see, now, I'd have never gotten her to ride back to that county seat where the real Lamonts were better known. Not without her slapping leather earlier, least-ways. Let's go outside. I may have mixed that battery acid a tad strong and these fumes make an unventilated cubbyhole sort of pungent."

Undersheriff Huston said he was glad it hadn't been just him fixing to bawl, puke, or both, as the three of them went back out on the side porch for some fresh crisp autumn air.

As Longarm offered all around and lit his own, Huston asked where he'd planned on spending the night, adding, "Ain't no hotel in town these days but we could put you up at my spread if need be."

Longarm shook his head and said, "Thanks all the same but there's no need. Cheyenne's sending their own deputy marshals to tidy up the loose ends. They'll take your word, as a lawman, about that shooting in your office earlier. I don't need you backing my need to gun a pair of obvious outlaws in the company of a known murderess, neither. After that I never saw them murder even the yard dog at the Lamont spread. So I'd be more in the way than a help as that Cheyenne team pokes about down yonder."

He enjoyed a deep drag, let it out through his nostrils, and added, "Meanwhile, like I said, the Denver District, with Cheyenne's blessings, wants me a good two days to the north, dealing with them charges of election fraud. So I hope to get a few miles in before nightfall and I can bed down most anywhere on open range, given a waterproof tarp to spread my bedding on."

The two older men exchanged thoughtful glances. Then Huston said, "That sun will be down, with a late moon rising, before you can get more'n four or six miles north of the river, old son. My old woman would be proud to steak and potato you and we've a real feather bed and plenty of quilts for overnight visitors."

Thinking Longarm undecided, he added, "Hell, you might as well stay 'til them other federal riders from Cheyenne show up. We got plenty of room, plenty of grub, and I'm sure them boys from Cheyenne will want to ask lots of questions about you, that mean old lady and her gang."

Longarm really had a time not looking away, or grinning like a shit-eating dog, as he replied in a desperately casual tone, "You may be right. But that's all the more reason for me to be on my way before anyone pesters me with all sorts of questions about details having nothing at all to do with the really criminal activities on or about that secluded homestead, pard."

Chapter 7

Longarm got off a last batch of less urgent wires, showed the postmaster how to drain the wet cells and rinse the plates off lest they corrode for no good reason before they were needed again, and still crossed the Sweetwater and a good six miles of open range by the time it was dark enough to give him pause.

He camped with no fire atop a brushy rise where neither the wind nor another gully washer was likely to harm him. Then he got an early start as a new day dawned crisp but sunny and calm.

A beeline from where he'd been to where he was going would just avoid the southeast corner of the big Wind River Indian Reserve. So he aimed a tad to his left, trending west northwest. He'd seldom had as much trouble with Indians on their reserve as the ones you might meet *off* it, and he was more interested in Indians, now, than when he'd first left Denver.

He still failed to see how any such folk could tie in with the election disputes up ahead. Quill Indians didn't get to vote in parts of the country where colored men and even white women might. But Billy Vail had mentioned rumors of Indian trouble up this way and he'd sure had some trouble with Indians, breeds, or folk who'd wanted him to feel he might have.

That reminded him to keep an eye on his backtrail as

he made his way across many a grassy rise and many a wooded draw without spotting anything more interesting than his pack pony behind him.

It was a good day's ride from the Sweetwater to the Agie River, where you forded into the fair-sized reserve set aside by the B.I.A. for the Washakie Shoshone and their Arapaho guests. So Longarm didn't spend as much time considering Indians ahead 'til he'd finished his noon beans, tomato preserves and cold coffee without incident.

Figuring that anyone following him had to be too good to spot and too shy to fight, Longarm told his ponies, as he was swapping saddles, "The Arapaho agent or mayhap that papist missionary at Saint Stephens might be able to give us a line on any newcomers speaking Chinook or Osage. All bets are off if some reservation kids have been getting frisky. They never tell white agents, priests, or even their elders when they're fixing to count some coup. We usually find out about it after they'd held the scalp dance or distributed the ponies to their in-laws, the sneaky rascals."

He rode on, nursing an after-coffee cheroot and admiring the ambition if not the brains of the big gray grasshoppers inspired by the unseasonable Indian Summer to keep whirring up on butterfly wings just ahead of him, as if they had no place else to land but directly in his path.

Thinking more, now, about where he was headed, Longarm mulled over the Indian question, past and present, this close to the east-west bottleneck of the South Pass Country.

The Washakie Shoshone had tried to avoid real trouble with their great father and been rewarded with a nicer reserve than some felt any infernal redskin deserved, including the core of their traditional hunting grounds extending out across the High Plains from the eastern slope of the Continental Divide to take in around twenty-five hundred square miles of rolling buffalo grass, timbered slopes and Alpine meadows to hunt summer elk in or even meet a Real Bear, as most Indians considered Mister Grizzly. If the buffalo were commencing to thin out, the B.I.A. made up the slack with government-issue longhorns and protected such friendly Indians from their more numerous enemies.

The so-called Apache resented Fort Apache down Arizona way and thought it was there to crush their hearts. But the pragmatic Washakie Shoshone seemed to take Fort Washakie, and the modest army garrison there, in the spirit meant by Secretary of the Interior, Carl Schurz.

Longarm found him a bit of a fuss, like President Hayes and Miss Lemonade Lucy. But Hayes and most of the new brooms he'd appointed to sweep up after poor old Useless Grant had done a good job. Longarm hardly caught any downright disgusting Indian Agents these days.

The part he liked best was that the Hayes Administration put such sons of bitches on *trial* whenever they got caught mistreating Indians. It almost made up for the current regulations about wearing suits and ties in court or not drinking openly in the same.

Longarm figured any trouble brewing on or about the Wind River Reservation was more likely to speak Arapaho than Shoshone. Arapaho were just like that. Even their Cheyenne cousins said that as soon as you put two Arapaho together you had three opinions. The band tucked into the southeast corner of the Wind River Reservation had claimed to be friendlies during, or at least right after, Little Big Horn. So they'd been taken in by the friendly Washakie Shoshone, with or without some army urging, and most of 'em had seemed to be getting along all right there, until lately.

Lately a splinter party of disgruntled Arapaho had accused the Shoshone of saying mean things behind their backs and petitioned their kindly old Uncle Carl, or *Mah-hah Ich-hon*, as some called him, for their own reserve, mayhap a tad larger than the Wind River Reservation, if that could be arranged.

Naturally it couldn't. Old Carl Big Eyes, as he'd been sensibly dubbed by Indians he was paid to keep an eye on, seemed a genuine reformer with a soft spot for the underdog. But he had to deal with a mostly Eastern congress and many a congressman from a more modestly proportioned Eastern state found it tough to believe a modest number of Indians couldn't get by on reserves as big or bigger than their home states. So there was already talk of cutting the Washakie Shoshone holdings down to just the twelve hundred square miles betwixt the continental divide and the Wind River, itself.

Longarm knew lots of white folk who'd feel mighty put upon by any government sassy enough to take nearly half their property away. But he was still betting on Arapaho rather than Shoshone trouble, if real Indian trouble arose at all.

But those riders against the skyline to the north of him didn't strike him as *any* sort of Indians as he just kept going, waiting for any one of the five of 'em to act more suspicious.

Longarm had been navigating by the sun rather than any trail across the rolling sea of shortgrass. So he knew they'd taken serious note of him when they swung his way, more thoughtfully than desperate.

They were about a mile out and closing casual when their bouncing hats dipped out of sight for the moment whilst they traversed a cross-grained draw. So he figured that as good a time as any to take out his wallet, unpin his federal badge, and stick it to the left breast pocket of his denim jacket. Then, just as five sombreros rose back in view, closer, Longarm and his own ponies crested a rise to move down the far side into a tanglewood of crack willow and chokecherry, eight to twenty feet tall and throwing plenty of tricky shade.

Longarm muttered, "Five on one is dirty fun and this must be the place." He reined in betwixt two willows, drew his saddle gun from its boot, and dismounted.

He tethered his stock there, where anyone really interested could spot sun-dappled horseflesh, sort of, and do whatever they had a mind to about it as they came over the far crest. Before that could happen Longarm had backtracked as far up the north-facing slope of the draw as any cover extended. He hunkered down in waist-high rabbitbrush and levered a round in the Winchester's chamber as he waited to see what happened next.

What happened next, it seemed to take a million years, was that the mysterious riders reined in along the far crest as if confused by all the shrubby stillness. One, standing in his stirrups, pointed about right at Longarm's half-concealed ponies and said something to the others that Longarm couldn't make out. Albeit he could guess.

Then another rider called out, louder, "Might we have the honor of addressing Marshal Long, from Denver?"

Longarm wasn't ready to give his own position away. So he yelled down at the dirt to his right, "I'm only a deputy marshal, but after that you got it right and what's this all about?"

He could tell by the way they were gaping about for him that his old hill country voice-throwing had worked. But nobody seemed too pissed off as the same voice replied, "We'd be riding for Sheriff Matilda Flanders, up the other side of Poison Creek. She sent us out to cut you off first and see you in safe the rest of the way."

Most men would have broken cover to act more relaxed by now. But Longarm wasn't most men and he'd been suckered by sweeter talkers in his time. So he called back, "Explain what you meant by cutting me off *first.*"

So the high-pitched kid voice speaking for the group called back, "Sheriff said she ain't clear on who else might be expecting you, or how come, but she still told us to get to you first. She said someone told her there was this breed, or mayhap a full-blood, packing an S&W .45 and dressed all in black, riding all over and asking all sorts of questions about you and when you might be expected. So, no shit, Longarm, do you want to play peek-a-boo all day or would you like us to carry you home for supper? We're going to have a time making her by sundown if we start right now, hear?"

Longarm studied some before he decided, "You boys ride on ahead and I'll follow, just out of easy rifle range, no offense."

The kid on the far crest sounded more astounded than offended as he called back, "Aw, come on, we got orders and why would anyone go through a whole heap of bullshit, at these odds, if doing you dirty was our intent?"

Longarm called back, "To improve them odds, for openers. I know I could be acting like an old maid, afraid to get in bed before looking under it. But you boys would be surprised what I've found under a bed before getting into it, now and again. I'd say it was a hundred to one you're telling the truth. But why take chances you don't have to in such an uncertain world?"

He threw his voice down at the dirt to his left this time, to keep them uncertain, as he yelled in yet another key, "If your sinister gunslick is real, and really out to get me, you boys can watch out for him just as good a quarter mile ahead of me on open range and I'll do the same for *your* backs if you should ride past any dry-gulchers hiding in a dog hole. So why don't we all get cracking, unless, of course, you ain't been exactly truthful with me?"

They argued some among themselves. Then their speaker yelled he really was an old maid, and ugly as well, before swinging his mount around to lead the general retreat.

Longarm let them retreat considerable before he broke cover to move down to his stock, swap saddles again, and mount up for one last standard but effective cavalry ruse. He rode down the draw a good two furlongs before he rode up the far rise with his Winchester braced across his lap. He saw the strangers who claimed to be deputy sheriffs riding just about where they should have been. He counted hats, twice, to make sure of all five. Most country boys who'd hunted crows, the kind that flew and et corn, knew the old dodge of having any number greater than three move into cover under observation so as to come back out the far side minus one. Smart birds and careless humans tended to see the differences betwixt one and two, or two and three, without counting. But once it got up around three or four, four or five, a body had to move his lips as well as his eyeballs to keep from being slickered.

He grew ever more certain they weren't trying to slicker him as the afternoon got later and they commenced passing range cows where buffalo had roamed right recent. He'd lost track of the unmarked southeast boundaries of the Wind River Reservation on his mental map, by now, because the riders he was trailing after weren't heading the way he'd originally meant to head. He knew everything north of the Agie and west of the Wind River was Indian land for certain and likely for keeps. How much land even friendlies might keep between the Wind River and Big Horn was as up for

67

grabs as the exact boundaries. The Big Horn Basin north of say Owl Creek was getting so settled you could hardly ride a full day between the sight of rising chimney smoke from one stock spread or another, and Miss Matilda Flanders wouldn't be running for a second term, just off to the east of the reservation, if the country in these parts hadn't gotten even more settled.

Wyoming was still a territory, run by a governor appointed from Washington and a legislature of local big shots, because most of it was still sort of empty, unless one counted Indians and cows as voting residents. But whether they'd settled in a state or territory, real voters were allowed to incorporate townships, and if need be counties, along the usual lines, going all the way back to the old country.

Western counties tended to be bigger than Eastern counties or the English shires they were modeled on. After that things worked much the same, with the county supervisor and other elected county officials running for office at the same times state and federal big shots had to.

Some held the word "Sheriff" had been brought back to England by crusaders back in Robin Hood's day. But Longarm spent lots of time at the Denver Public Library near the end of each month when his pocket jingle was running low. So he knew an A-rab Sharif was only a cuss claiming kinship with Mohammad by way of his daughter, Miss Fatima.

The old Anglo-Saxon for Sheriff had been "Shire Reeve," a reeve being an overseer, guardian or peace officer. Each township or "Hundred" as old-timey folk might call it, had its own reeve with the shire reeve riding herd on 'em and answering to the crown for law and order in his shire. But as anyone who'd ever read about Robin Hood knew, that shire reeve or Sheriff of Nottingham hadn't been voted in by the common folk in them parts and that's what the American Revolution had been all about.

American sheriffs were supposed to get their jobs fair and square in fair and square elections, after which they were free as any Sheriff of Nottingham to deputize or hire all the help they wanted. The voters would let 'em know in the next election whether they approved or not.

At least, that was the way it was supposed to work. Longarm had seen enough of the way things *really* worked to just about give up on democracy as soon as he could come up with any system that didn't seem ten times worse.

It was a shame he didn't know those riders out ahead of him way better. For they said they rode for the she-sheriff about to get herself elected again, or vice versa, and he still wasn't clear as to why she felt the need for outside help. The boys up ahead seemed able to ride crosscountry without falling off and the spokeman he'd jawed long distance with had acted sensible enough. If they were really out to escort him safely in.

Each mile they led him on seemed to make that more likely. Outlaws out to do a lawman they knew by name would hardly be riding ever closer to where he'd be safer than them, if that was the way they were riding.

Longarm decided to study on that before trusting anyone at those odds when he saw them reining in for a trail break. He reined in on a rise to dismount and change saddles again a good half mile away. Then he watered himself and both ponies, lit a fresh smoke, and stayed afoot to rest his butt and both their backs while he morosely watched the distant riders for hostile moves and tried to figure out where in blue blazes everyone might be.

He'd *intended* to find his way to Saint Stephens with the help of Beaver Creek and the Little Popo, which came together pointing smack at the mission run by mostly French Canadian priests to save Arapaho souls. Protestant missionaries had never had as much luck with Quill Indians. Longarm had no idea why, either.

From the mission near the south boundary of the big reservation he'd intended to follow the combined waters, now the Agie, northeast to where it ran into the Wind River and ask further directions from anyone he met on the far side of, say, Poison Creek. He knew the new pro tem county seat called Medicine Skull had to be somewhere betwixt the headwaters of the Poison and the Badwater. But the rascals who'd been sent to fetch him, they said, seemed to have beelined way to the southeast of his chosen route, and he was confused as hell about the many draws, some watered and most dry, they'd crossed getting this far.

When he saw them remounting in the distance to ride on he had little choice but to follow, reflecting that, on the bright side, others as strange to this range would hardly be expecting a Colorado rider to be approaching Medicine Skull from this particular direction. So as soon as you studied on it, those boys were carrying out their orders pretty good, if that was what they were doing. He wasn't about to give them a crack at doing anything much until he knew them better.

The sun was low and the rolling range seemed to be getting a tad higher by the time Longarm was starting to hurt for another trail break or at least a piss call. But you saw less timber or even brush in the draws winding mostly northwest towards the Sweetwater and Big Horn, now.

Longarm knew why the tawny country all about looked so dry despite its altitude and latitude. He'd thought Billy Vail was joshing that time he'd been ordered to go to Hell, mayhaps a stage stop or so from where he'd been sent this time. Folk in these parts of the High Plains hadn't named so many settlements so grim because they'd all been reading Edgar Allan Poe on their way west. Things got dubbed Hell, Despair, Poison, Badwater and such by discoverers discouraged by the natural alkali salts of range something mean had happened to back in the time of them giant lizards you still found traces of up this way.

Since then a heap of rain had cleansed the soil deep as most shortgrass, soapweed and such rooted, while saltbush could manage in the deeper alkalied draws, offering bitter but safe fodder even as it warned man and beast not to drink any nearby water. The ground water was good enough for tree roots and even human consumption in other parts, albeit not even the Sweetwater flowed soft enough to get suds with your average soap, so despite all the gloomy things it was called, the Wind River Country, as it was known in general, made a swell place to raise beef, if only someone could do something about all those *Indians* squatting on the best parts of it.

The sky above was turning pumpkin and the sunset was starting to gild the shortgrass tips all about when Longarm topped a rise to spy lots of lavender woodsmoke against the royal purple to the east. Some of the windows were already lamp-lit in the low ramble of sod or frame buildings ahead. Longarm was tempted to catch up with the others as they all forged on into what just had to be the town of Medicine Skull. But he never. He'd once had a bad border tough waiting for him right in the lady's bedroom instead of the alley, patio and other rooms she'd led him through with such innocently wicked smiles.

But once he'd let the five riders precede him all the way in and saw all the townsfolk they were mixed in with, now, Longarm decided he might have misjudged the boys.

He said so, sheepishly, when he reined in close enough for a fair view in tricky light of the statuesque blonde talking back to them from a veranda waist-high to the dirt street. She was wearing a gilt star as well as a man's work shirt over her heroic breasts. Her ample hips were girded by a split skirt of Indian-tanned deerskin, fringed but not beaded. Her waist seemed waspy for the ample curves above and below. The fine-boned face staring up at him from betwixt straight braids of flaxen hair, parted sort of Arapaho, seemed neither too young nor too old for a grown man to kiss. It was tougher to tell, by this light, whether a man ought to or not. She said, "Call me Matt and tell me why you've been acting so suspicious of my deputies. Didn't they tell you I'd sent them to meet you because I had reason to believe someone might be gunning for the both of us?"

Longarm nodded pleasantly as her boys, who really did seem mere boys, up close, as he calmly replied, "Anyone can call himself a deputy sheriff, Ma'am. I had to shoot two strangers claiming they were someone they weren't just to get this far. They might have had some Indian blood. You say there's someone who seems Indian for certain, saying mean things about me in these parts?"

Sheriff Matilda Flanders turned to a man standing nearby in a striped shirt and white apron. She told him to tell Longarm about the stranger who'd been asking about him. The obvious barkeep shrugged and said, "He drinks pretty good and wears his six-gun tied down, too. I never said he said anything *mean* about you, if you'd be the one and original Longarm, Mister."

Longarm dismounted as he asked what the mysterious cuss might have said if it hadn't been mean.

The barkeep replied, "Just that he'd heard you was headed this way and that he wanted to meet up with you, bad."

"He wasn't one of our regular Shoshone or Arapaho," another townie cut in, adding, "I tried saying howdy to him both ways. He just smiled at me, sort of superior, and allowed he was neither sissy breed."

Longarm asked if the proud stranger had said what nation he might hail from. Sheriff Flanders answered for him, saying, "Osage. He was heard by others, making the same brag. Let's put those ponies away for you and talk about it over supper. Someone must be sore as hell at the both of us if they're sending all the way to the Osage Strip for hired guns!"

Longarm handed over the reins and lead line to one of the kids he'd been so suspicious of as he removed his saddle bags and Winchester, muttering half to himself, "I did get a wire on a bad Osage called Black Wolf. He might be introducing himself as Jerry Shunkaha Sapa if he's all that proud about his nation."

Nobody there had any reply to that. Apparently the morose black-clad Osage had been asking more questions than he'd been answering.

Matilda Flanders said, "Follow me this way," but he followed her walking way less she-male around to a flight of outside stairs and up them to what seemed commodious quarters on the top floor.

She agreed, when asked, the chambers below made up her office and modest county jail. She said she had nobody locked in her patent cells at the moment, waving him to a horsehair sofa as she added, "We used to get more for our drunk tank, this close to payday, before I showed 'em I meant what I said about disturbing the peace around here. My kids can handle that sort of trouble. I sent for you because it may take a man to handle a man-sized showdown before this is over."

He leaned his Winchester in a corner and placed his saddlebags on the floor by the sofa before he hung up his hat and sat down, softly asking, "Do you really think a lady of your obvious breeding ought to indulge in man-sized showdowns, Miss Matt?"

She snapped, "I was fixing to coffee and cake us. Would you rather fight me bare knuckles, winner take this badge?"

He chuckled fondly and replied, "I already got a badge, Ma'am, and I know nobody with a lick of sense expects the county sheriff, his or herself, to take on all comers. That's what they give folk like you and Marshal Billy Vail deputies for. It was *you*, just now, who raised the issue of showdowns, man-sized or any sized."

She sighed and said, "I'm sorry. You're right. I'm getting testy and taking it out on others but . . . damn it, they're just not being fair!"

He asked who *they* might be, not having a name, so far, to go on.

She bleakly replied, "The ones who gunned my husband, the original Sheriff Flanders, of course. I put this badge on, days later, when not another man in the county would even touch it. I know at least some of them were threatened by the same people who dry-gulched poor Bob. But try to get anyone around here to *admit* it!"

He whistled softly and asked, "What about those kids you sent out to fetch me?"

To which she replied with a sigh, "You're right. They're kids. The powers that be don't seem to want grown men, or even grown women with a law library getting in their way. Excuse me. I'll be right back."

It took her more like five minutes and he dammit hadn't had time to ask her permit to smoke before she'd dashed back to her kitchen. So he wearily rose for a closer look at the law books she'd just mentioned.

She, or more likely her late husband, had amassed enough books for a modest law office on some shelves above a sideboard at right angles to the sofa. He could see by the covers that most of them had been read, more than once. But of course he couldn't tell whether the real sheriff or his widow had been trying to memorize all that law.

A good lawman had to have more book learning than a heap of good old boys thought. There was more to being a good sheriff, or even a town marshal, than simply being halfway tougher and a tad braver than your average asshole.

Not knowing that was what had made so many town-tamers bad lawmen as well as dead ones. But as the late James Butler Hickock had proven in more tough towns than one, folk were more impressed by a pistol whipping or, better yet, a killing, than they were by professional peacekeeping for, by definition, there was nothing to brag on, come election day, when a true professional kept anything all that wild from *happening*.

So why was someone acting so wild about a she-sheriff running for the first time after being appointed to fill out a dead husband's time in office? The way *sensible* rivals would be most likely to beat her would be by leaving her the hell alone.

She came back in with a tray of German silver heaped with sweet pastry and bitter black coffee. She asked him if he'd shift a bitty table of cherrywood closer to the sofa for them. He'd just gotten up to do so when someone else commenced pounding on the door out to those stairs. She put her tray down and moved to open it with a puzzled frown. Longarm put a casual hand to the grips of his .44-40 as she opened it.

But the kid deputy in her doorway looked more scared than scary as he gasped, "He's back! *Two* of him, this time! Both asking for Longarm here, and I fear someone must have told them he's in town, from the determined way they seem to be waiting, down in the Alkali Saloon!"

Longarm reached for his Stetson and put it on as the she-sheriff murmured, "Wait 'til I get my own sidearm and I'm going with you."

To which he could only reply, "No you ain't, Miss Matt. I ain't being brave. I'm being sensible. I work best alone in a serious situation, and this one sounds sort of serious."

Chapter 8

She-sheriffs didn't listen any more than any other women.
So she followed Longarm and her kid deputy all the way
down those stairs with a Walker hogleg riding cross-draw
on her right hip.

She was either left-handed or had a lot to learn about
gun-toting as well as gunfights. But Longarm forgave her,
some, when they were met by two more of her deputies
at the bottom of the steps and one of 'em declared, "The
barkeep's gone down to the cellar to inspect their rattraps
and all the regulars left early for whatever reasons. So them
bad Injuns are alone at the bar and we got both the front
and back doors covered."

His sidekick chimed in, "We're just waiting for orders
to storm the Alkali and teach them bad Injuns some manners!"

Longarm shook his head and said, "Not before I've had
a word with 'em, or tried to, leastways. We won't know
whether they're good or bad before we give them the chance
to show us, hear?"

The she-sheriff he'd been trying to shuck all the way
down those stairs told her boys, "Deputy Long's in command, for now. I sent for him because he's an experienced
lawman who's dealt with this sort of nonsense before."

The kid who was all for storming the saloon replied,
"Them old boys waiting on him in the Alkali look more

serious than nonsensical, Miss Matt. They're packing double-actions in tied-down cutaway holsters and muttering mean to one another in their own lingo every time someone passes on the walk out front!"

Sheriff Flanders looked a mite older and a heap paler as she turned to Longarm to ask, "Wouldn't it be safer for all concerned if we let them know they were surrounded and ordered them to come out with their hands up?"

Longarm shrugged and replied, "They might not want to, and there's no way to call a bullet back once it's on its way to the target. So I like to know who the target might be before I let fly any bullets."

The five of them were moving along the dark main street toward the Alkali Saloon now, as one of the kid deputies who'd first met Longarm out on open range observed, "You wasn't half as considerate of us white boys this afternoon as you seem to be about two redskins you don't even know!"

Longarm smiled thinly and replied, "I didn't know who you were or what you wanted when first we met up, so uncertain. I hope you recall I didn't open fire on any of you, either. For I'm sure you'll agree that could have led to needlessly disgusting results."

Sheriff Flanders brightened and declared, "I see what he means. Had he opened up on you without waiting to make sure you'd have doubtless fired back."

Longarm nodded soberly and said, "Just as any two gents trapped in a taproom and ordered to surrender by a person or persons unknown might be inclined to. So we'd best do it my way."

They did. When they joined the larger party covering the lamp-lit doors and windows of the rinky-dink saloon from the dark, outside, their she-sheriff ordered everyone back to maximum pistol range lest the morose individuals inside take heed of them and get even more proddy. An old boy who'd just peeked through the batwings said they seemed to be staring about uneasy as they waited for that barkeep to come back up from the cellar.

Longarm told them he was going in by way of the back door and not to act trigger happy 'til they knew what they

76

thought they were doing. When he told Matilda Flanders to stay put, this time, he put enough iron in his voice to make his words stick. So he was already feeling lonely as he eased between two shops shut down for the night into the dark alley behind them and of course the saloon.

Writers such as Ned Buntline and Crawford of the Denver Post were already writing gunfighting tales more dramatic than accurate, and both had vexed Longarm in the recent past with guff about him being the fastest draw in or about Denver.

He knew he could get his gun out quicker than your average outlaw because he was still alive after six or eight years with the Justice Department. But a man packed a pistol on his hip so as to have it handy when and if he might need it, not to engage in dangerous athletic contests with those he wasn't at all fond of. So, knowing he could be walking into trouble, Longarm had his double action .44-40 out and trained the way he was headed as he eased up the back steps of the saloon and opened a screen door as gingerly as a schoolboy feeling up his first sweetheart.

A floorboard creaked under him in the dark corridor leading to the lamp-lit main room. So one of the two strangers standing at the bar was staring right at the bead curtain screening the back way out as Longarm froze in place, hoping those shiny beads were screening him as well.

The strangers looked Indian enough to be pure bloods, and their six-guns were worn as serious as described. But while both wore black, high-crowned hats, their duds were old Army issue, redyed with something darker and doubtless cheaper than the original Army blue. Old Army issue faded like hell, exposed to the brighter sunlight and harder water west of the Big Muddy.

Suspecting he knew who they were riding for, and hoping like hell he'd guessed right, Longarm lowered his six-gun politely to his side and called out he was coming before he popped through the bead curtain at them.

Neither went for his gun. Longarm kept his own pointed down at the sawdust-covered floor, letting the badge on his

chest do some talking for him as he soberly said, "I understand someone here would like a word with U.S. Deputy
Custis Long?"

The older of the two morose-looking Indians nodded
in a more relaxed way and said, "We sure would. I'd be
Sergeant Shunka Inyankey or Running Dog of the Osage
Police. This is my pard, Corporal Sintey Luta or Red Tail.
We heard you'd worked with our outfit a spell back and
our boss said you are one Wasichu Wastey, or decent pale
face."

Longarm chuckled fondly and replied, "I try to be, whenever you red devils let me. But what can I *do* for you red
devils, seeing you've already ordered them beer schooners
Indians ain't supposed to, according to Washington."

Running Dog looked disgusted and said, "I hear
Washington died of an ague he caught riding through
a rainstorm to get laid. We're after a real red devil called
Shunkaha Sapa. You're more likely to have him down as
Black Wolf."

Longarm nodded soberly and said, "We got him listed
both ways. We ain't all greenhorns. I know the charges and
I have heard he might be out this way. That's all I know.
So it's your turn."

The somewhat younger Osage called Red Tail volunteered, "We got a tip he'd boasted of some gal he had out
this way with more Wasichu blood and the know-how to
blend in, on or off the B.I.A. blanket."

Running Dog nodded and said, "Black Wolf looks more
Wasichu than us and you're right about it being easy enough
to order liquor as long as you know how to dress up
and behave. She seems to have him dressed more Mex
than Osage but, after that, she'd been far from a civilizing
influence. They've pulled off half a dozen robberies since
first we got a lead on them being this far west, less than a
month ago."

Longarm thought, then shook his head, saying, "If you
boys have heard I'd brushed with outlaws who could have
been breeds, forget it. Neither of the old boys I shot it out
with could have been more than a quarter anything but trash
white, and they spoke more Chinook than Osage. As to the

gal they were working with, she looked like an old Wasichu lady. Is that how Black Wolf's doxy gets described?"

Running Dog shook his head and answered, "Young and pretty. The murderous rascal likes his women young and pretty whether they want him or not."

That reminded Longarm of a no-longer young but still pretty blonde. So he said, "We'd best continue this discussion in company with the local law, soon as I let 'em know this wasn't what it looked like. I don't suppose you boys would like to show me some identification before I put this old piss-oliver away and call the others in?"

The two Indian peace officers looked more startled than insulted. Then Running Dog got out his wallet with a grin, saying, "I was wondering why you still had the drop on us, however polite. Don't you ever take anything on trust, Wasichu Wastey?"

Longarm waited until he'd examined the other lawman's federal badge and I.D. before he soberly replied, "Not when I don't have to. Sometimes I have to and it's scared me shitless more than once."

Chapter 9

Most Wyoming folk thought a woman in the main room of a saloon more shocking than male Indians drinking in one, wearing pants. So neither Sheriff Matilda Flanders nor her senior kid deputies commented on the beer schooners in front of the Osage lawmen as they all took a corner table to get sorted out.

She'd sent all but the three kids Longarm had talked to earlier off to bed, or wherever kid deputies went after eight or so. Longarm wanted to ask how come she had those kids deputized and behaving so eager if she couldn't get any experienced lawmen to work for her. But you had to eat any apple a bite at a time, and the two grown Indian lawmen sounded more interesting at the moment.

Matt Flanders listened with as much interest as Longarm related his Indian or part-Indian adventures on his way up from Denver, save for the naughty parts that hardly seemed to prove anything one way or the other. She agreed with Longarm that nobody he'd brushed with had described as the notorious and described-in-depth Jerry Black Wolf. She said she'd gotten her own all-points wire and asked about. She added that nobody within a day's ride had owned up to harboring or even spotting anyone who might have been an Osage trying to pass for a breed or Mex.

Running Dog nodded soberly at Longarm and said, "That's why we were looking for you, Wasichu Wastey.

We don't think he's trying to hide out among Wasichu in country so thinly settled by anyone. We think he might be on the blanket, pretending to be a reservation ward among the hills and dales of that big Wind River Agency."

Longarm started to say something dumb. Then he nodded thoughtfully and decided, "Shoshone and Arapaho have to speak English to each other as well as to the few troopers and B.I.A. folk. If he's got either a local Shoshone or Arapaho doxy with him she'd know which he'd want to say he was when they met up with anyone, and you're right about all them hills and dales. The bureau's got a handful of clients rattling around a swamping amount of mostly empty wilderness, from shortgrass rolling prairie to a good imitation of them Swiss Alps."

Matt Flanders seemed to forget who might be sitting there with her as she girlishly growled, "That's way too much land for so few fool Indians. It was dumb of them to spoil the Washakie Shoshone like that just for being timid when those others rose against us back in the seventies."

Running Dog just glowered. The younger Red Tail muttered, "Hear me, my nation took scalps, Wasichu scalps, *many*, during the fight between the Blue Sleeves and the Gray Sleeves. Nobody rewarded us with more lands in the Indian Nation for being *timid!*"

Before the she-sheriff could put another foot in her mouth Longarm told her, "He means the Osage fought Cherokee and other Confederates for the Union, Miss Matt. He's right about Washington feeling grateful and feeling the fool Cherokee deserved to lose at least that much of their original allotment. As for the closer Shoshone in more recent times, some Shoshone did ride against us in '78, along with Bannock and such. I was there. So I can tell you how good it felt to hear the big Washakie band had decided to sit that one out."

Turning back to the Indians he continued, "She's right about that being one big reservation, though, and I can't say I know it all that much better than you boys. So what *can* I do for you in connection with your trackdown? Billy Vail never sent me up here after anyone called Black Wolf, you know."

Running Dog said, "We don't want you to help us track him all the way down. We think with winter coming on he'll have to hole up somewhere. Somewhere the people who know the country better might be able to suggest to us. But we are Osage, not skittish Arapaho or Shoshone diggers, and you know how some people blame us for fighting Cherokee for you people, that time."

Longarm smiled crookedly and suggested, "For openers, don't ever call a Shoshone a Digger Indian. Utes and Bannock don't cotton to it, neither, even if they do speak the same lingo as the root-digging and rabbit-eating Paiute, who'd *rather* be called Tohono or Ho."

Running Dog shrugged and said, "Anyone who talks like a digger is a digger in my book. Be that as it may, we've heard you have a way with diggers or, have it your way, Ho. They don't run away when they see Wasichu Wastey coming."

Longarm said, *"They* call me *'Saltu ka Saltu,'* or 'the stranger who is not a stranger,' likely because I make some effort to get along with 'em, just as I try to be nice to you Sioux."

Both Indians sucked in their breaths and Red Tail said a terrible thing about Longarm's mother in their own lingo. It was Running Dog who said, in English, "Bite your tongue! We are Osage and Sioux is a dreadful thing to call anyone, even those Nakota, Dakota or Lakota you've had so much trouble with. I would tell you what Sioux means, in Chippewa or Ojibwa, if there was not a woman listening."

Longarm insisted, "Lots of folk insist, scientifical in books, that you Osage, Omaha, Iowa, Hidasta and so on talk Sioux, the same as the Lakota or Serious Sioux."

"That's not fair!" protested Red Tail. "We may speak the same way but we have nothing in common with those killers and thieves, nothing!"

Longarm shrugged and said, "Do tell? Seems to me I heard something about a Sioux-speaking Osage wanted for killing and robbing folk of various complexion. My point is that you got to draw the line the same place for everyone and Shoshone don't cotton to being dismissed as diggers any more than you Osage like to be classified as Sioux. Try and keep that in mind as you visit the Wind River Agency, boys."

Running Dog grimaced and said, "It's not that simple. Diggers or, all right, Shoshone can be just as rude to strangers and we're on *really* bad terms with Arapaho. We used to fight them and the South Cheyenne before Washington marched the Cherokee west to give us some *real* enemies to fight."

Red Tail smiled wistfully and said, "I enjoyed it when we got to fight Cherokee. They're good fighters. There's a lot of brag in a Cherokee's scalp!"

Running Dog silenced him with a warning look and told Longarm, "We want you to ride over to Fort Washakie with us and get us started. We think the Shoshone Police might help us if someone they trusted told them we were all right."

Matt Flanders frowned and murmured, "Durn it, Custis, you just got here and it was *me* who sent for you, remember?"

He nodded soberly and said, "I never say I'm going somewhere before I know I have to go there. I sent some wires out of Split Rock, yesterday, saying I might be here in Medicine Skull by this evening if anyone had anything to wire back. So before we get into a dumb argument, here, let's go over to your Western Union and see if there's any more on that wayward Osage outlaw and his doxy."

They all drained their beer schooners and rose to get cracking, with one of those kid deputies leading the way.

Seeing he had the time, Longarm asked. The she-sheriff explained none of the eight or ten regular deputies she'd managed to recruit since her husband's murder had reported being threatened and she had no call to feel any had been bribed.

That just added to the mystery of all her husband's original help quitting when she'd been appointed to fill out his term. None of them had ever seen fit to explain just why. None of the older men she'd tried to recruit had said right out they were afraid to take the job or unwilling to work for a woman. But she felt certain it had to be one or the other.

The Western Union was down toward the other end of town, so there was time to ask who was running against her in the coming election. He found it hard to buy when she told him neither opposition party had announced its full slate, yet. She said she thought they ought to get cracking with the elections about to start any day now. But he cocked a brow to demand, "Did you just mention more than one party, Ma'am?"

To which she replied, "Democrat, Republican and Granger. The other incumbents, like my late husband and me, would be Granger, of course."

He muttered, "Of course," but didn't feel half that sure, as they all strode on. Nobody seemed to know for certain whether The Grange was a political party or an agrarian society. A disgruntled farmer and tax reformer named Oliver Kelley had organized his National Grange of the Patrons of Husbandry right after the war to eat cucumbers and perform other wonders. They'd grown like ragweed during and after the financial depression of the seventies and sent legislators to the capitals of Illinois, Iowa, Minnesota and Wisconsin, to crack down on the railroaders and storage outfits. Some of the so-called Granger laws were likely to stay on the books, being way more fair to folk who worked the land, and they'd even put up national candidates in the last election, which Hayes and his Reform Republicans had won instead. Since then a lot of country folk had dropped out as business got better and old Oliver Kelley talked wilder about collective farms and cattle cooperatives. It wasn't so surprising a she-sheriff had been appointed by a county commission of such progressive folk.

It was easier to see, now, why more mainstream voters might not want to sign up with a utopian political movement that seemed to be fading away like that Cheshire cat Miss Alice had met in Wonderland.

Medicine Skull wasn't all that big. So his political musings had to be set aside when they got to the Western Union. As Longarm bellied up to the counter with the others in tow he learned he'd guessed more than right about there being some

84

messages waiting for him. The clerk handed over a bundle.

But nobody, anywhere, had a thing more to say about the wicked Jerry Black Wolf. A marshal up Salem way opined the darker of the two sneaks Longarm had gunned at the Lamont spread answered to the wants on their own bad breed, a part Klamath and mostly German boy called Billy Weismann. Any Oregon rascals he'd lit out with would have been as likely to savvy Chinook jargon.

There was a shorter message from Marshal Vail, chiding him for not reporting in more often, but warning him not to send anything at nickel-a-word day rates unless it was important.

A terse reply from Marie's Crow Agency made even less sense. It thanked him for letting them know where one of its wards had wandered but added they'd been missing no such person. The only Marie Mato Wastey they'd ever heard of had just drawn her provisions, this being the end of October and all.

So he had to laugh like hell when he read the wire from the sheriff's department down in Rawlins. When Matt Flanders asked why he chuckled some more and explained, "They're holding this gal I used to know as a horse thief. A smart as well as honest horse trader thought to check with the remount officer at nearby Fort Steele when she tried to sell him some stock. One was an army bay last seen headed north in concert with a male Wasichu, namely me. I'd best let 'em know she helped herself to that gelding with my blessings if not my permission."

But he never. For, reading on, he was able to make even less sense of a homesick Absaroka gal's conflicting tales of woe, until he snapped his fingers, turned to Running Dog, and said, "Absaroka is as close to Osage as say Mexican Spanish to Cuban Spanish, right?"

The Indian lawman blinked and answered, "If you say so. I don't savvy either. But I guess I could get through to a Crow if I had to."

Longarm said, "She speaks English good as us in any case. Could you boys make Rawlins, down along the U.P. tracks, this side of Monday?"

85

The Indians exchanged thoughtful glances. Red Tail said something too fast to follow in Osage. Running Dog nodded and told Longarm, "If we started right now with fresh ponies. But what's the hurry and what are we supposed to do when we get there?"

Longarm said, "You ain't supposed to hold a suspect more than seventy-two hours without pressing formal charges. But weekend days don't count if you don't want 'em to. The idea is to let her go with apologies instead of suspicions she might be being followed. I'll be sending detailed instructions to Rawlins by night letter. So you boys will be told exactly when they'll be letting her go after getting word from me I never wanted to press charges."

He turned to the bemused she-sheriff to say, "You'll swap these fellow lawmen fresh stock from your own remuda so's they can be on their way, won't you, Miss Matt?"

She nodded but said, "Provided you'll tell me why."

He said, "Wastey. I'll be proud to tell you all about it once we send these boys on their way. I'm sure they'll be professional enough to extend professional courtesy when they file their official reports on an important federal arrest. Ain't that right, boys?"

Running Dog nodded in a mighty puzzled way and said, "We'll write you up for an assist, if only you'll tell us what you're assisting us with."

Longarm said, "Not me. Miss Matt, here. I ain't the one running for county sheriff most any day now."

Chapter 10

Small town folk raised country style didn't stay up late as they might have in Denver or Dodge. So Medicine Skull lay mighty still all around by the time the moon was up and those Osage Police were off for Rawlins.

Longarm had let Matt read the night letter he'd composed for the lawmen holding that confounding Absaroka gal. But she confessed she was still confounded as she led him back to her combined quarters and county jail.

He said, "I reckon you'd have had to have been there from the beginning. Do you mind if I smoke, Ma'am?"

"For heaven's sake we're on a public walk," she replied, adding, "You can spit, for all I care, as long as you aim off the planking. Why don't you start at the beginning, with you and that Indian girl."

He reached for a cheroot as he sighed and said, "Going back to the very beginning a wayward Absaroka and likely part mountain-man gal who might have been named Claudette, not being Marie Good Bear at all, lit out from the Crow Agency, dishonest, whether before or after she met up with an even wilder Indian called Jerry Black Wolf."

Matt nodded and said, "They'd have had both English and their native dialects in common, right?"

He lit his cheroot without breaking stride and said, "Reports on 'em robbing folk said they discussed their next best moves in some Indian lingo. We knew which one Black Wolf spoke. So add that part up and let's get to when they spotted me, alone on open range with more horseflesh, guns, trail supplies and who knew what all."

Matt frowned thoughtfully and said, "But you told us, before, you'd met just that girl, friendly. Would you care to tell me just *how* friendly, Custis?"

Longarm snorted smoke out both nostrils and answered, "Let's say friendly enough to sell me a treasure map to Casper Ferry, where they'd been coming from instead of going, most likely. They had me down as greener to the high country than I was. So I spotted her and threw down on her when I sensed someone creeping in on me, Indian style. Her true love, Black Wolf, lit out to reconsider his options when he saw how good I was. From his yellow sheets he's never been one for a fair fight in the open by broad day."

Matt said, "I remember the wanted fliers on the mean thing. Get back to that mean squaw, and how mean she might have been to you when she found herself at your mercy!"

He chuckled and replied, "Aw, I didn't know she was at my mercy. The tale she told made sense to anyone who hadn't heard about Black Wolf traveling cross-country with another assimilated Indian. They'd dismounted well spread out, doubtless to have me in their cross fire once old Jerry had worked up his nerve. Looking back, I can see Miss Mato Wastey had more nerve than many an owlhoot rider I've met up with, bless her innocent smile."

"Then she *did* get naughty with you!" the somewhat older and less naughty-looking blonde declared, as if that had any bearing on any damned federal warrant.

He sighed and said, "I was under the impression I was saving us both from a fate worse than naughty, the more fool I. Like I said, they'd left their own ponies off a ways to creep in on me. When I let her go fetch her own paint she likely had time to signal Black Wolf at some distance. All the horse nations use the same sign lingo. I reckon their plan was for him to circle wide and for her to sucker me into a tight ambush. Like I just said, they'd likely been over the country ahead of me before I could get to it."

Matt marveled, "Good heavens, how did you ever escape with your hair?"

To which he could only modestly reply, "Easy. As I told Miss Mato Wastey, I'd scouted for the cavalry up this way in my mispent youth. So I was more used to being ambushed on rolling shortgrass than your average Wasichu. I set a greenhorn course to let anyone out there plot our destruction by twilight in any ambush site of their choosing. But then I zigged when they expected me to zag and sent her paint on alone, knowing its white patches would show up farther out in the dark than the rest of us."

The she-sheriff dimpled demurely and speculated, "You must have surprised Miss Good Bear as well. So tell me, how good was she?"

He kept his own tone detached, though it wasn't easy, as he said simply, "I ain't sure such an adroit fibber had all that much good *in* her. I'd say her evil companion was suspicious about *my* morals as you seem to be, no offense. For after he'd waited quite a spell after dark for the two of us to show up, he blasted that poor paint in the tricky light, suspecting she'd been indulging in tricks with a chosen victim. I can't say whether he just fired and ran or ran when he saw what he'd done and suspected she'd really changed sides on him."

Matt said, "I can follow your logic up to a jealous Indian gunning his sweetheart, or her horse, and after that you lose me completely. Didn't I just hear you tell those Osage Police that Crow girl would almost surely lead them to her true love once they let her off on that horse-stealing charge?"

He let out some smoke and agreed, "You sure did, Ma'am. For whilst it's true she might have just been streaking for home, reformed, on the one army bay she'd purloined with my blessings if not my permission, she was trying to unload *two* ponies in Rawlins when they arrested her. They only charged her with stealing the army bay because, to date, not a soul's come forward to claim the roan mare she'd offered as well."

Matt nodded soberly and decided, "She circled, searching for him, after parting company with you, and I see it all better, now. They not only made up, they decided to get out of these parts by rail, far and fast!"

He said, "That's about the size of it. The law down in Rawlins has of course been holding both ponies as well as her and all her cash and possibles. So it seems almost certain her traveling companion holed up, nearby, to await further developments. She'd have told him I wasn't likely to press charges and that it'd be safe to sell that army bay before she got picked up trying to sell it, see?"

She laughed and said, "I do now. Had they arrived in Rawlins with enough train fare to matter they'd have never chanced leaving business records that might lead someone slick as you to the railroad ticket office."

He shrugged and said, "He needs her to do some of his talking for him, too. She ain't as squawlike as you seem to picture her and, by the way, no nation that don't speak Algonquin cottons to having its gals called squaws."

"What did _you_ call her—'Honey Bunch?' " the she-sheriff demanded in a mocking tone.

He laughed easily and replied, "Not hardly. Getting back to catching crooks, Running Dog and Red Tail agreed to write you and your county up for helping 'em catch Black Wolf and _his_, not _my,_ honey bunch. That ought to garner you a vote or more if the capture hits the papers in time."

She brightened and said, "I know. That was very sweet of the three of you, Custis. But will it be fair, to _you_, I mean? Seems to me you could use that assist on your _own_ arrest record, right?"

He said, "Wrong. I've already made enough arrests for a raise in rank and pay if only I wasn't already a senior deputy and President Hayes hadn't got in on a sound money and budget-balancing platform."

They were almost to those stairs leading up to her quarters by this time. He assumed she meant to get something from her office down below when she led him past it and unlocked the street-level door instead.

As they groped their way inside the dark front office she asked him if he'd mind stroking another match for the lamp he'd find over that sort of spooky black mass, adding, "It's awfully late and I'm sure you're about ready to be tucked in for the night."

He'd been ready since about halfway through that coffee and cake upstairs. But he still struck a light and saw she'd been talking about an oil lamp hanging above a big oak desk in the center of the front office. As he lit and trimmed the wick the soft light glowed landlord green on the bars of the patent cells, four of 'em, lined up in the back. They were called "patent cells" because the rolling mill that made 'em in kit form had patented the design. They were shipped flat and bolted together once they got where they were going, mostly to small towns, albeit even some big city jails found the combination of boilerplate walls and vanadium steel bars right handy.

Each patent cell came with fold-down bunks and built-in sinks and crappers. But as the she-sheriff swung open an unlocked door of floor-to-lintel bars she warned him, "The plumbing hasn't been hooked up yet. I mean to deal with that as soon as the elections are over, if I win. You know how unwise it can be to let out three-figure contracts just *before* an election and, meanwhile, there's the facilities we've *been* using, through that door marked 'private,' by the gun racks."

He said he'd keep that in mind and asked, with a puzzled smile, "Are you saying I'm to spend the rest of the night down here on a cell bunk, Ma'am?"

She nodded soberly and replied, "I know what you're too polite to mention. I do have more than one extra bedroom upstairs. But how would it look if a hitherto respectable widow woman openly cohabitated with a young and handsome stranger?"

He sighed and said, "It could surely cost you more than one vote. I thank you for calling me handsome and strange, Ma'am. But I sure wish I hadn't drank all that black coffee, earlier."

She looked away with an odd little smile as she replied, "The blankets on all four bunks are clean. We haven't had much business here since the fall roundup. If it gets too cold for eight blankets feel free to light that potbelly in yonder corner. You'd be surprised how much heat it can

91

throw and . . . Well, I'd best leave you, now, before anyone across the way wonders what I'm doing up and about at this hour."

So they shook on it and parted friendly. But as he held the front door open for her she couldn't resist murmuring, "I'm sorry I drank all that black coffee, too!"

Chapter 11

The blankets were hardly Hudson Bay, but they were way warmer that your average county jail kept on hand. So once he'd piled 'em all on the bottom bunk at one end of the cell block and trimmed that oil lamp he felt no need to light that stove, even sleeping bare-ass. Albeit, by the time he'd hung up all his duds and slipped his goose bumps atop two and under six wool blankets he could feel the coming winter pussyfooting through the frame walls, boilerplate and thin dry air all around him.

Black coffee could do worse than keep a man awake, albeit it was doing that, too, as he kept jerking awake every time his tired frame commenced to go all-the-way limp.

What was worse, as he kept trying to drop off and the night kept getting colder, was that he was commencing to feel like pissing. He knew he'd surely wake up before morning from one of those annoying dreams where ladies you didn't know well kept popping in on you just as you were about to let fly, and that he'd freeze his poor balls blue rolling out to piss icicles, unless he got up right *now* and got it over with before it got any colder.

On the other hand he was feeling so snug right now and he'd surely fall asleep before he really had to get up and . . .

"Let's get it over with and not have that dream about that sewing circle catching you in the act of watering that Boston fern!" he told himself, sternly, as he tossed the covers off before his weak flesh could change his waversome mind.

A weaker-fleshed man might have never made it on bare feet with a bare ass to that door marked "private" by the gun racks. For, thanks to that coffee, he'd apparently been lying there longer than he'd figured, and the night, even indoors, had cooled to just plain frosty.

He hadn't thought to tote along any matches. But there was enough moonlight coming through the one bitty window for him to aim at the white stoneware urinal and he did so with a sigh of pure pleasure despite the way the rest of him was shivering.

There didn't seem to be any mechanism for flushing. But, judging from the smell of fresh pine tar and stale piss, you weren't required to.

The bitty corner sink worked, sort of. He managed a stream of cold water no stronger than he'd just pissed and dried his hands on his own hair in lieu of any towel. Then he put a damp hand on the icy brass knob to prepare for his dash back to those warm blankets.

Then, just outside the closed door, all hell seemed to be busting loose as at least one shotgun and a couple six-guns blazed away at something or someone, close!

Longarm felt goose-bumped indeed as he could only stand naked and unarmed in the dark behind such thin door paneling, hoping hard nobody would peg any of those rapid-fire rounds his way.

Then, a million years or at least a dozen shots later, it seemed to be over. The shooting just outside had stopped and he could make out doors and windows opening all around in the middle distance.

That didn't mean he was about to stick his nose outside before he had at least an educated guess as to what all that gunplay had been about. For like many a country boy he'd hunted woodchucks enough to know what could happen to any critter dumb enough to stick its head out for a look-see while someone with more patience and a reloaded gun was hoping for just that.

He'd left his own guns with his boots and duds in that damned old distant cell, of course. For who packed a six-gun to the shithouse when he thought he was all alone? There were riot guns neatly arrow in that gun rack just outside. Sure there were. Locked in place and doubtless empty. Maybe he could open that bitty window over the commode?

He couldn't. Not without tools, or cutting the shit out if his bare hands, thanks to the sons of bitches who'd painted over the frame so many damned times. So what *else* might he try? There wasn't even an inside bolt on this damned door. That she-sheriff doubtless used her own facilities upstairs and kids didn't care who watched.

He heard boot-heels clunking a lot. He couldn't tell whether they were coming or going. He started to call out, but decided it might not be his turn as, outside, someone struck a match to light up his bare toes and the floorboards down there as they got that oil lamp going some more.

Then a familiar voice gasped out, "Oh, dear God, not again!"

So he called, "I'm in here, Miss Matt."

He hadn't expected her to just yank open the door with a vastly relieved smile, wearing little more than a night robe and that six-gun. He'd been right about her being a southpaw.

From the way her amber eyes saucered as her smile turned to a little pink O, she hadn't expected to catch him wearing nothing at all but goose bumps.

His freshy drained organ grinder was hanging down between them as limp as it ever got, but she still let out the gasp of a schoolmarm finding a snake in a desk drawer as she slammed the door shut again and bleated, "For Heaven's sake, I thought that was you piled in a corner of one cell. I'll get your things. Don't you dare come out of there before you've put some clothes on! The whole town's staring in here from outside!"

He allowed that didn't surprise him when she next cracked the door open just enough to toss in everything from his boots up at his bare feet. She shut the door again without answering. But as he quickly dressed he heard her telling someone out there that they'd assassinated yet another lawman.

He didn't know who *they* were and felt assassination was a mite strong until, strapping his gun rig on over his denim-clad hips and stepping out of the shithouse, he smelled all that gunsmoke.

Two of Matt's kid deputies had come in to help while others stayed out front to keep the townsfolk from cluttering up the scene of the crime.

The who and why were more mysterious than the how. Longarm stepped into the cell he'd been trying to sleep in and shook the piled blankets out, one at a time. As bullets and buckshot clinked all over the cement floor he decided, "A .45, a .41 and Number Nine buck, meaning at least three of 'em or an octopus with mismatched guns. These blankets ain't as badly shot up as I'd have been if I'd been wrapped in 'em. You still have your front glass, too. Yet I locked up before turning in. So how many keys might we be talking about, Miss Matt?"

The she-sheriff sighed and asked, "Would you like that alphabetical or numerical? Aside from just about everyone in my sheriff's department, some of the county help, and anyone who's ever had a chance to borrow a key for a few minutes . . ."

"I follow your drift," he cut in, moving back toward the desk as he continued, "I noticed it was one of them simple spring locks, no offense, you could open with a hat pin if you really wanted to."

As he reached up to trim the overhead lamp she asked, "Don't you mean if you were a woman who knew how to pick a lock with her hat pin?"

He doused the lamp, turning all the faces pressed against the front glass to inky silhouettes as he calmly replied, "They do say things happen in threes, Ma'am. But I can't see you sending all the way to Denver for me if you never wanted me here in Medicine Skull."

There was still enough moonlight shining in above the heads of the crowd outside to make one another out, sort of, as she protested, "Not *me*, you goof! That Crow girl and her Osage lover! What if you guessed wrong about them

96

being bound for . . . Oh, that's right, she's in jail down in Carbon County but he . . ."

"Wouldn't be in these parts, after me, even if I sent them Osage boys on a snipe hunt," he cut in, adding, "I admire your imagination, Ma'am. But even if Black Wolf had doubled back on his trail we know he's a treacherous sneak with a yellow streak."

The she-sheriff gazed around the dimly lit interior as she asked, "What would you call what just happened, *heroics?* Let's assume they were brave enough to come this far inside. From hereabouts you can see into all four cells, and all but that one bunk lie stripped to the mattress ticking."

Longarm nodded morosely at the dark shapeless form the eight piled blankets made on that one bunk and opined, "I'd figure that might be somebody, too, if I was expecting somebody in here, alone, and snuck in to see nothing better in sight. But Black Wolf won't work unless we certify him as feebleminded, Miss Matt. Most of the town already knew I'd sent them Osage Police somewhere else entire after Black Wolf and before that everyone had him streaking for that nearby Indian Agency. So why would he want to offer the law a fresh crack at his trail from here, even if he had the grit?"

Matt frowned thoughtfully and said, "He, she, or they ran away on foot after that hasty fusillade. I was half asleep but still awake, just upstairs, when they opened fire right under me. I'd have noticed hoofbeats or even boot-heels running along the plank walk out front. So that means, Good Lord, they have to still be right here in town!"

It was Longarm's turn to make sardonic comments about alphabets and numbers as he glanced at the huddled masses on the walk out front. Some had already drifted away. Only the more curious were inclined to hang around the scene of some excitement, this late, with nothing at all exciting to gape at.

Longarm started to ask the exact population of Medicine Skull, then put that question near the back of the stove, as he reflected on how many country folk and wayfaring strangers, good or bad, could be in a given trail town on any given night.

To the she-sheriff's credit, it was one of her kid deputies who asked if they were fixing to posse up. Matt Flanders sighed and asked him, "To what purpose, Jimmy? We don't know what they looked like, which way they went, or even how many of them there might have been."

The kid insisted, "It stands to reason any strangers we find out on open range at this hour might have something to hide, right?"

It was Longarm who gently explained, "Lots of folk have lots to hide, Jimmy. Elected peace officers who make a habit of stopping just anybody at any time without probable cause don't get reelected as often. That's one of the few advantages of living in a democracy."

"Then how in thunder were you figuring on catching the rascals?" the boy demanded, as if he thought Longarm knew.

Longarm didn't fuss at him. He'd been a boy, one time, himself. So he just said, "I doubt we will, unless they try again, and I win."

Chapter 12

After all had been said and done, Longarm still got to sleep by midnight, albeit a mite on the sly.

Not wanting to press his luck any further in that jail cell, and seeing he still hadn't been invited upstairs, he waited until he was alone again to slip over to the livery for a quiet word with the old colored man on night duty. Then he got his own bedding out of their tack room and spread it atop the springy shortgrass hay in the loft above the pony stalls. The hay was mostly buffalo and greasy grass, but there was enough sweet-smelling love grass mixed in to make him glad he'd thought of this. More than one pony nickered and all of 'em stirred as he climbed up the ladder. So he figured that even if he hadn't tipped that old hostler enough he'd be safe up yonder if he kept his duds on and his guns handy.

By this time that earlier coffee had about worn off. So the next thing he knew it was cockcrow. He let the literal cocks crow 'til he just had to get up and drain his own, again. Then he washed the gum out of his eyes at the hand pump he'd found out back by their shithouse and smoked a spell with the old colored gent as they watched the sun come up, out front.

Longarm had found in his travels that next to small town barbers there was nobody like the local colored folk to fill a lawman in on local gossip, as long as they'd decided he was all right. So that was another reason to treat most everyone he met all right. Grown up white folk tended to talk as openly in front of kids and colored help as they might in front of critters. Longarm came right out and said this as he lit both their cheroots in the chill morning air. The older man laughed mellow but weary before confiding he'd noticed that, even though his freedom would have been old enough to marry up with if she'd been born a real Miss Liberty of the right complexion.

Longarm asked him to consider the alternatives and continued, "I told you last night who I was, Mister Jackson. You might as well know I'm up here looking into complaints of improper voter registration."

The colored hostler said nobody had asked him whether he wanted to vote or not. When Longarm asked him if anyone had told him he wouldn't be allowed to he simply shrugged and said the thought had never occured to him since he'd left Texas a spell back, riding drag on one of those Goodnight-Loving drives.

He said, "Some gents of color down home signed up to vote right after the war, Captain. Them gents who come down from the north promised forty acres and a mule to any freedman who'd vote the way they said. But nobody never got nothing but tar and feather, or worse, in the end."

Longarm blew smoke out his nostrils and observed, "Reconstruction was rough on everybody, and I've forgiven President Hayes a heap, knowing he saw fit to scrap all that bullshit as impractical. Getting back to the here and now, up this way, I'm trying to decide if the Democrats, the Republicans, or Sheriff Matilda Flanders herself, has been confused about due process and properly conducted election proceedings."

The old hostler said he'd heard customers of the Democrat persuasion accusing Republicans of dirty doings, and vice versa, whilst others, including members of her own Grange Movement, seemed to think Miss Matt just needed a man to set her mind straight with a good stiff dick.

The old colored man hastily added, "Don't nobody go saying it was *this* old darky saying things like that about any white widow woman, Captain. I just repeating what others said, like you asked me to!"

Longarm smiled assuringly and said he hadn't been entertaining such thoughts about their she-sheriff, either. There were times a little white lie seemed called for.

When he asked whether his informant had heard anything about more suitable recruits being threatened in any way if they signed on as deputy sheriffs the old timer shook his head but said, "Some say she's accused 'em of that. Duke Duncan, her husband's senior deputy, tossed his badge at the country board when they appointed her instead of him to fill out her dead husband's term. A dozen others who'd ridden with Sheriff Flanders under Duke resigned about the same time."

Longarm didn't ask why. He said, "I reckon I'd feel put out if someone shot Marshal Vail and they appointed someone from the typing pool down the hall to boss me around. But you're sure nobody's come right out and threatened lesser lights willing to serve under a she-sheriff, Mister Jackson?"

The hostler laughed that same weary mellow way and replied, "I know this is likely to come as a surprise to you, captain. But this pickaninny ain't never been invited to wear no deputy's badge. I have heard Duke Duncan and some other have refused to drink or play cards with any of Matt's new riders. But that's as ugly as it's been, so far, as far as I know."

Jackson didn't know why the county board had chosen even a pretty widow woman over an experienced deputy, either. So, seeing he'd been invited for breakfast by said widow, once it was broad day and nobody could accuse anyone of night crawling, Longarm handed the older man another cheroot to last him 'til his relief showed up, and ambled back to the county jail to see what she-sheriffs served on such crisp sunny morns.

She must have been watching for his coming for when he got to the head of those outside stairs she'd already started to fry sausage and wheat cakes. As she let him in he saw she'd put a fresh apron on over a summer-weight Dolly Varden of figured muslin, with her bodice buttoned up the back tight enough to show more curves than skin.

She took his hat and sat him down to stuff him and coffee him as she offered to change back into her riding habit if he wanted to ride out and scout for sign.

He said he'd rather canvas suspects right in town until he had a better handle on what he was supposed to expect. Had that bodice been cut looser, or thicker, he'd have wondered why she'd put it on to breakfast with a man she wanted to go riding with. When she murmured something about taking a picnic hamper along to the rise Medicine Skull had been named for, he naturally found himself asking what they were talking about.

She said she'd thought he'd known the town was named for an Indian holy place where nations had agreed in the Shining Times to respect one another's hunting rights.

She added, "The sacred buffalo skull they swore on is back east in some museum, now, of course. But the sort of wagon wheel they laid out with white quartz is still there, if you're interested."

He was, to some extent. He knew the site had been important to the Indians indeed if they'd bothered with rocks from that distant. You could rustle up shale and sandstone in the closer foothills. But to gather white quartz in quantity you had to get way up in the Wind River Range, where the spine of the continent busted through a mile or more of younger sedimentary rock. So he washed down some sausage and asked if that ancient treaty had involved white folk.

She shook her head and poured more syrup on a second helping he wasn't sure he had room for as she replied, "It all took place so long ago not even the Indians know all the details. We think Shoshone and Crow agreed to something or other, there. They'd started fighting again by the time the first mountain men came out this way, before either of us could have been born."

He made a wry face and said, "I reckon it don't matter to either nation, now. We'd be just about astraddle the drainage to the Big Horn and Powder, here, right?"

She nodded and said, "We drive such beef as we have to ship to the rail line, five or six days to the south, as cows walk without losing weight. Once we get all the grass as

102

far west as the Wind River we suspect the railroaders will see fit to lay more tracks up this way."

He cocked a brow and replied, "I suspect they would indeed. But this is the first I've heard about stealing a good third of that Washakie Shoshone Reserve."

She dimpled and said, "Oh, Custis, nobody said anything about *stealing* land from any Indians. I'm sure they'll be offered a fair price and it's not as if they're *doing* anything with all that open range on our side of the Wind River."

He forced himself to swallow a polite amount of his second helping. It wasn't easy. The first one had been six thick slabs of wheat cake slathered in store-bought salted butter and sorghum syrup. He washed down some sausage as well before musing aloud, "Well, Lord knows the Lakota Confederacy wasn't mining all that gold in the Black Hills and they'd have been better off taking the money and letting Custer keep his hair. Have either Shoshone or Arapaho been making faces at white folk over all that range they couldn't have any use for?"

She shook her blond head and seemed sincere as she replied, "As a matter of fact they seldom hunt on our side of the river, now that the buffalo have been thinned out up this way. Bob never had any trouble with reservation Indians when he was alive and that mean Osage my boys and me never laid eyes on seems to be as wicked an Indian as we've had in these parts for a couple of summers or more."

He managed to recall without asking that her man, the Sheriff Flanders the voters had really elected, had been a Robert, or Bob, before he'd been dry-gulched. He didn't ask her about that, either. He'd read the report on his way up from Denver. He figured few women would want to talk about a husband who'd been spread across the bottom of a dry wash a good three days before anyone but carrion crows, coyotes and all sorts of bugs had found him. They still had the same county coroner. He'd be the one to ask about any grim details they'd skimmed over. On paper it had said he'd been blown out of his saddle, then finished with a head shot, at closer range, by the same .52-210 buffalo gun, likely a Hawken or Leman. The autopsy report

Longarm had seen had included neither a photograph nor diagrams. But it was safe to assume there'd been enough of the skull left to identify. A .52-210 was designed to knock a full-grown buffalo off its feet. The effects on a pumpkin or a human head could be upsetting to one's survivors.

He knew he'd have heard about it, by now, had she had any notion as to who'd dry-gulched her man. But there'd been nothing in that report about a disgruntled senior deputy called Duke Duncan. So he asked her about that instead.

She sighed and said, "I've always called him Lewis, since that's his Christian name. He and Bob were on the best of terms, of course. Would *you* make an enemy your senior deputy?"

Longarm shook his head and said, "Not if I knew he was my enemy. How come he got so sore at you if him and your man were such pals?"

She lowered her lashes and murmured, "Perhaps he wanted to be my pal as well. He'd deny it, now, of course, and to be fair he never got forward while I was still in mourning. But more than one here in town has said he always seemed sort of sweet on me, in a decent way, of course."

Longarm didn't argue as he held up an after-breakfast smoke for her approval before lighting up. She nodded and said, "Call me vain if you like, but I suspect Lewis Duncan just couldn't abide the thought of serving under a woman he'd been planning on . . . you know, serving in other ways? What is it about you men that *we're* supposed to take orders from a lover but it's a deadly insult if ever the shoe should wind up on the other foot?"

Longarm finished what he was doing, shook out the match and exhaled before he replied, "I can only speak for myself, but I follow your drift and mayhap there *is* something wrong with us. I've been offered jobs, good jobs, by pretty ladies with more money and maybe more power than my ugly old boss man. More than one has even offered to support me in a manner I might enjoy getting accustomed to with no effort required on my part."

The she-sheriff smiled archly, blushed becomingly as she recalled the night before in greater detail, and decided, "I imagine they had some chores around the house in mind for

104

you. But of course you were too proud to ever take orders from a mere woman, right?"

He started to deny her accusation. Then he smiled sheepishly and said, "I don't think of women as *mere*, Ma'am. I reckon it's because we're brung up to admire men who protect and provide for women whilst looking down on those few grown men who live off or under 'em."

He saw he might have hurt her feelings. So he quickly added, "Duke Duncan might have acted so rude because he liked you even more than he let on, Ma'am. Them urges some of us feel for members of the opposite gender, or even our own, can mix us up just awesome."

She turned a brighter shade of dusky rose as she softly replied, "I know. Where *did* you spend the night, by the way? I took some warm chocolate downstairs to help you sleep, once all the excitement had died down, and I have to say you gave me quite a start when I found you gone."

He smiled thinly and explained, "I thought it best not to mention where I meant to spend the rest of the night. I'd been startled all I wanted to be, for one night."

Then he tried in vain to catch her eye as he continued in a more meaningful tone, "That just goes to show you how stupid any man can act around a halfway pretty lady."

She dimpled and rose to clear the table, sounding mighty flustered as she thanked him for calling her pretty and agreeing natural feelings could sure make people do stupid things.

She proved it a few moments later when, after helping her pile the tableware in her kitchen sink, he put a natural hand around her surprisingly slim waist to reel her in for a howdy kiss.

She almost decked him. A lesser man would have surely gone down and in truth he was staring bemused through pinwheeling stars as he grabbed both her wrists and hung on for dear life before she could swing again. For the Junoesque blonde threw a wicked left hook, better than many a male brawler's, and her right arm seemed impossibly strong as well to a man who could only hang on, gasping, "Simmer down, Miss Matt, you've won and I surrender unconditional, see?"

105

Then she went suddenly limp and began to bawl like a little gal lost in the woods. So he hauled her too close to fist fight and refrained from any wrestling holds that might have scared her as he soothed, "Aw, hush, I meant no harm, I'm sorry if you thought I did, and let's say no more about it, Miss Matt."

She buried her face in his chest to sob, "I don't know why I just did that, Custis. I *wanted* you to kiss me. But then, when I knew you were about to kiss me . . . I must be going crazy. They say being alone after you've gotten used to regular loving can do that, right?"

He patted her back, resisting the impulse to unbutton her tight bodice, as he soberly replied, "I ain't sure I've ever gotten it as regular or gone as long without, Miss Matt. I don't suspect you of insanity. You're a bright, pretty lady with more worries on her plate than average. You got every right to feel confounded about men and other mysteries. So why don't we just take it easy and worry one step at a time?"

She laughed weakly, clung more strongly to him, and asked him what he found so mysterious about his own gender.

He chuckled back and said, "Nothing. It's womankind I'll never understand if I live to be a hundred. Men and women deserve something better than one another. But we're what we're stuck with. The Lord, or Mother Nature, designed us to be horny and fruitful. It didn't matter whether we enjoyed ourselves, total, as long as we couldn't leave one another alone no matter what our common sense told us."

She laughed again, dirtier, and said, "My common sense and my other parts have been arguing about you all night, as well you must have known, you poor confused thing. I've been trying not to involve myself that way with any man, 'til after the election, at least. Do I have to tell you how gossip is liable to affect the results in a territory where even the old biddy hens have the vote?"

He chuckled and said, "You'd resent it if it was me wondering about any sort of she-males voting. But you're likely right. Lots of old *men* can't abide younger folk having more

106

fun than they can. Once you go into politics it's tougher to get away with romance than it is to get away with stealing. That's likely why there are so many crooks and so few lovebirds in politics."

She sighed and said, "I know. What are we going to do about us, Custis?"

He knew what he *wanted* to do. But he really liked her. So he said, "It depends on how bad you want your job, Miss Matt. Putting it pal to pal, a pretty gal can always get laid, before or after she runs for public office."

She laughed incredulously and said, "I should be more shocked than I feel. Is that a promise, Custis?"

He put a gentle hand to her chin, tilted her head back, and bent to kiss her, mighty friendly, before he told her, "Meanwhile I've been up here long enough for a leisurely breakfast, some quick slap and tickle, but hardly both. So why don't I get back outside where everyone can see me, fully dressed and breathing easy, in less time than it takes to gossip about a lady?"

She said she wasn't sure she cared. He told her she would be if it cost her many votes and that, meanwhile, he really had other fish to fry if there was anything to her suspicions about election fraud.

He told her he'd be back around noon to take her up on that picnic out to Medicine Skull Rise. So he was damned if he could figure why she'd busted a coffee cup against the door as he was closing it after him.

Chapter 13

Longarm wasn't sure he needed a haircut and felt no pressing need to trust his throat to any total stranger with a razor in such uncertain surroundings. But next to barbers and invisible colored help there were few who heard more small town gossip than a job printer who put out a boilerplate on the side. So that made as good a place as any to start.

A boilerplate, according to Crawford of the Denver Post, was one of those rinky-dink weekly newspapers devoted mostly to paid notices extolling the virtues of local brides and hardware establishments. A page or more might be hand set with local news. But to save on time and the expense of full-time reporters they sent away for preset national or even regional news, which reminded some insiders of heavy boilerplates.

Gilt lettering on the glass of their front door bragged on a five-digit circulation figure for the *Medicine Skull Monitor*. Longarm took that with a grain of salt and went on in to see what else they might fib about.

He was surprised, not unpleasantly, to find a brown-haired gal in an ink-stained denim smock sticking type and apparently in charge of the whole shop. She came around the big slanty type case, still holding the type in her stick with an ink-grimed thumb, to belly up to the far side of the counter barring the general public from the working parts of the modest-sized shop. He figured her a mite older, up close, but no more than thirty, give or take how long she'd been engaged in such honest toil.

Longarm had taken his badge off and put it away again the night before, of course. So she got to look a tad surprised and just as likely disappointed when he flashed his open wallet at her and told her what he was doing in her town.

She held the paragraph or so of type she'd been setting higher as she told him, wryly, "We heard, Deputy Long. Uncle Frank feels you're worth eight or ten lines, if only to keep that silly widow Flanders from charging another cover-up."

He smiled thinly and said, "Uncle Frank would be Franklin W. Flint, Proprietor, and you'd be, what, a Democrat or Republican news organ, Miss . . . ah?"

She said, "I'm Ida Flint and we're not prosperous enough to have any editorial policy. I suppose if push comes to shove we've a few more readers registered as Republicans than Democrats, depending on whether they sell yard goods or beef. But the Grangers and independents will probably tip the scales to the same nonentities we've got running the townships and county now."

Longarm frowned thoughtfully and said, "I have been wondering how come nobody but Sheriff Flanders has called for impartial outside help, charging someone from at least one of the other parties in these parts of . . ."

"Of nothing," Ida Flint cut in, flatly adding, "Neither the Democrats nor Republicans have nominated anyone to run against her this fall. So in just a few days she'll be running unopposed for her second or in point of fact first term."

Longarm put his badge away as he decided, "Well, I swan if I don't find this a tad confounding, Miss Ida. This is an election year. The office of Sheriff is one of the highest in your average county and with her on such shaky footing . . ."

"Matilda Flanders is standing solid as Pikes Peak," the print shop gal cut in, sniffing as if she'd just smelled something burning as she continued, "A lot of folk feel they *have* to back her, if only to spite the killers who

109

dry-gulched her man. A lot of the womenfolk who get to vote in these parts are mighty proud to see one of their own kind in such high office and to give her her due I suppose she's done all right since they appointed her to wear her husband's badge."

"But you don't like her," Longarm said, more certainly. It had been a statement rather than a question. But Ida smiled wanly and confided, "Maybe I'm jealous. Or maybe I'm afraid she's going to mess up and set us all back another generation. She didn't have to start all this guff about padded registration records. They handed her the job on a silver platter. She has the budget she needs to keep things running smoothly in such a thinly populated and generally law-abiding community."

Longarm allowed he'd been reading up on all the crimes they'd been reporting up this way. He agreed that save for the murder of the one and original Sheriff Flanders business had been sort of slow.

He asked what she could tell him about the charges Bob Flanders's widow had been making. Ida shrugged and said, "You'd better ask Uncle Frank or, better yet, her. I just work here. I do recall Uncle Frank saying he thought she was likely getting queer from spending too much time alone, late at night, with just her worried mind for company. He said he'd looked into what she'd said about dead folk coming back to vote this fall, but hadn't met any, personally."

Longarm made a mental note to pin Matt down to more specific charges when they got back together, later in the day. When he asked, Ida Flint said her uncle was out collecting subscription money. She suggested he try later in the afternoon, adding they locked up around six.

He headed next for the County Courthouse, in hopes of hearing more sense from someone on the County Board of Supervisors. When he got there a funny little gal with hair to match those fuzz-balls you find under beds assured him he'd been correct in assuming they had the usual county organization, in this case a reform coalition made up of Grangers, Democrats and one Progressive Republican.

110

Then she spoiled it all by confiding that while all the lesser lights were doubtless hard at work, somewhere about, all the big shots, including the County Supervisor in the flesh, had knocked off a mite early in order to combine some political fence-mending with their usual noon dinners.

That sounded reasonable, with the election just next Tuesday and payday coming up. So Longarm headed for a reasonable place for a small town politico to have his noon dinner, as soon as one considered how many votes he was apt to swing at *home*.

The Alkali Saloon was way more crowded that morning than it had been the night before. When Longarm bulled his way to the bar, with some effort, and asked if they could aim him at County Supervisor Burnett, even though he was flashing his badge an almost as tall and heavier-built gent grabbed his gun arm, downright rude, and asked who wanted to know.

Longarm swung around to stand almost nose to nose with the other man, who was dressed as cow but not as clean. His breath smelled as if he'd been brushing his teeth with sardines soaked in bourbon as the barkeep warned, "Take it easy, Duke. The man just said he was the law and his badge reads federal."

So Longarm knew who he was dealing with as Matt Flanders's former deputy snarled, "I don't care if he thinks he's President Fucking Hayes. I'm still waiting for him to speak when he's been spoken to!"

Longarm smiled as pleasantly as the situation seemed to call for and softly said, "Consider yourself spoken to, Lewis. And let go my arm. I mean that."

The man who preferred to be called Duke Duncan blinked, glared, and snarled, "I see you been talking to Matt Flanders and you'd better cut that out! By rights old Bob's badge was mine! Maybe her, too, if only she'd face up to her true feelings as a woman."

Longarm snorted in distaste and asked, "Hell, why dream so modest? Why not replace President Hayes and get his Lemonade Lucy to knock off twenty pounds and start serving hard liquor again at the White House. I've seen her in

111

the flesh and she's as likely in love with such an asshole as well."

Then he grabbed the wrist of Duncan's gun hand as it headed about where he'd expected it to. It wasn't the first time someone had tried to slap leather on him whilst clinging to *his* gun arm.

As more than once voice warned, "Oh, shit!" and the crowd moved back to give them more room, Longarm knew he had two choices. He took the least lethal course. Knowing he was strong enough to break free, and what that was likely to lead to, as two armed men wound up facing off at point-blank range, Longarm kindly kneed Duke Duncan in the groin and hung on to that wrist as the poor bastard went down writhing in agony.

They wound up more or less together on the sawdust floor, with Longarm seated comfortably on Duke's chest as he twisted the moaning bully's six-gun out of his hand and hit him with it a few good licks to calm him down.

As he rose from the unconscious Duncan's spread-out form with the single-action thumb-buster in his own big fist, backward, he could tell the action had provoked mixed reactions from the Medicine Skull boys. Some seemed to feel Longarm had done a long overdo good deed while others opined old Duke was all right, leastways when he was sober. Nobody seemed to want to take up his fight where they'd just seen it left off.

As Longarm handed Duke's six-gun across the mock mahogany to the reasonable barkeep, an older and way better-dressed gent stepped up to him to declare, "I'd be T. B. Burnett and why don't we talk about it more private, in a back room, Deputy?"

That made more sense to Longarm, too. As he followed the county supervisor back through those same bead curtains he remembered they were joined by two leaner and meaner-looking gents dressed to remind Longarm of a lot of professional gamblers and not a few hired guns he might have met up with in the past.

He knew they weren't going to sit down to play poker when Burnett introduced them as his private bodyguards. Longarm didn't ask how come. Someone had already shot the county sheriff and the kid deputies he'd seen so far didn't look as if they could guard an apple orchard against more determined kids.

But there was in fact a card table in the back room they wound up in. T. B. Burnett sent one of his older boys back to the bar for some refreshments instead of cards, as the other held his chair away from the table for him, as if he were a lady.

Longarm sat his own butt down across from the county supervisor. The bodyguard left remained on his feet, facing the door with a self-assured expression and the ivory grips of a Colt Lightning peeking out from under his frock coat.

After some small talk about Duke Duncan, with Burnett voting to have him charged with attempted suicide, if nothing else, while Longarm was for giving him another chance, they got down to more important concerns.

Longarm wasn't surprised to learn the county supervisor and some of his fellow board members were a mite annoyed at the opposition for *not* running anyone against a really swell but mayhap flighty she-male, next Tuesday.

Burnett confided, "I don't recall who nominated her to fill poor Bob's boots when they first brought him in, all shot to shit. But I did second the motion and I meant it, at the time."

He offered an Havana across the table as he continued, "I figured she could use the money and I knew it would be a popular political move at the moment. But that was then and this is now and how were we to know she'd take her job so serious, or *permanent*?"

Longarm accepted the cigar but asked, before he lit it, what Matt Flanders had done to unsettle her own party so.

As he was working on getting the fancy smoke going the politico who'd put Matt in office explained, "She's done a better job as our sheriff than we had any right to expect. Duke Duncan wasn't the only old pro who refused to serve under a woman. The kids she had to replace them with would be pathetic if she was as dumb. But she's not dumb and if she lacks some fighting skills she more than makes up for it by knowing so many of the town and country folk she was to cope with, and how they think. She's handled

113

domestic violence like a strict but understanding big sister, and you know more than half of all serious crimes take place betwixt folk who used to be fond of one another."

Longarm nodded and said, "That's likely what makes 'em so serious. I'd hate to see that asshole, Duncan, trying to break up a domestic dispute. But I'm missing something, here. You ain't the first to sing faint praises of Matt Flanders, here in Medicine Skull. So exactly who might be bitching about what, here?"

Burnett said, "We can't get her to shut up about some mysterious sons of bitches being out to steal the election from her. Don't say it to me. Tell *her* there's nobody running against her! She can't seem to get it through her head that she has to win if nobody else but *herself* drops a ballot in one box for her!"

That other bodyguard came back with a pitcher of beer but only two glasses. Longarm would have offered both bodyguards a sip, at least, on duty or not. But he wasn't paying them. So he just sipped suds and went on smoking as Burnett explained, "The opposition hasn't seen fit to go after Matilda's position, this time out, because it's smarter to leave popular incumbents alone and concentrate your strength where the outcome is less certain. You've probably noticed I don't make as favorable an impression as the widow Flanders. Don't make excuses for me. It's a fact of nature and I'm good as I am at the game because I do look in the mirror and I try to see myself as others see me."

He took a drag on his own cigar before he sighed and said, "A beefy baby-kissing glad-hander who may not steal us blind as long as we keep an eye on him. I *said* I look in the mirror. But I didn't want to go into the family undertaking business, and an ambitious lad who looks like a typical party hack can inspire confidence the same way a gambler who looks like a typical gambler does. Do you have any idea how?"

Longarm nodded and said, "By making sure you're dealing dead on the level once you have everyone at the table watching you like hawks. I met Bet A Million Gates one time. Looks like he'd sell gold bricks to his own mother. But he still gets them as know him to bet against him.

114

He's *paid* millions on those occasions he's lost and, so far, nobody has ever caught him cheating."

Burnett nodded smugly and said, "Damned A. I've been in politics all my adult life and they've never caught me with my hand in the till yet. I switched from the Democrats to the Grange ten years ago when I saw how many voters who'd ridden for the North had yet to forgive the Rebs or Copperheads of that particular party. I'm not ready to go back to them but as you must have noticed, the Grange Movement has been ebbing fast since it almost swept into national power back in '76."

Longarm blew a thoughtful doughnut of expensive smoke and replied, not unkindly, "I'd have trouble voting the straight Granger ticket next Tuesday, if anyone on Earth could *explain* it to me."

Burnett nodded soberly and said, "If you're going to be radical you have to remain consistent. A lot of big farmers and stockmen who were attracted to our standing up to the Eastern banks and business trusts have been mighty upset by soapbox screaming about fixing prices and soaking the bigger landholders."

Longarm nodded sagely. "All isms seem to appeal more to the one getting the free lunch than the one paying for the cold cuts. You boys promised so much to so many that it seems you've attracted a mighty mixed bag."

"With the reputation we'd as soon let the anarchists and such keep and cherish for their very own!" The Granger sighed, adding, "That's why someone has to talk some sense to Matilda. If we Grangers can just hold on long enough to join forces with the less radical members of the labor movement, there'll be no stopping us by the end of this century."

Longarm didn't answer. He was more worried about that she-sheriff than the future of her party. But Burnett droned on, "We're thinking of calling ourselves the Populist Party, standing for the common man working in a factory or on a farm. Meanwhile we're going to have to dump the red radicals who preach the sharing of wives and the blowing up of public buildings. So about Matilda and these crazy charges of hers . . ."

"Someone gunned her man," Longarm cut in, adding, "Last night, someone tried to gun me. Unless we assume that was her, both times, Miss Matt can't be the only one thinking wild around here!"

As he started to rise, Burnett insisted, "Wait, damn it. I never said nobody could be out to do our county sheriff dirty. I was there when they brought poor old Bob in. It's just that until we know who and what's behind all this other madness she's not helping us at all by sounding off with mad charges of her own, see?"

Longarm got to his feet, saying, "I'm commencing to. I'd best go see how mad her charges sound to me as I take 'em down in more detail."

Chapter 14

It was well before noon and he still found the she-sheriff waiting with a picnic hamper. She'd changed her riding duds and donned her left-handed gun rig as well. But Longarm bulled her back inside when she met him at the top of her stairs. He said, "First things first and Medicine Skull Rise will still be there after you and me are long gone, Miss Matt."

He fished out his notebook and waved her to a seat in her own front room as he continued, "I've come all the way up here from Denver and while everyone agrees something murky must be going on I've heard more backing and filling than facts. More than one I've talked to this morning seem as confounded as me. So let's get down to brass tacks. I want some names. I'll settle for one name you'd care to charge with doing something unconstitutional."

She'd already dropped gracefully to that same sofa as she replied, "I told you last night. I've reason to believe someone's been fudging with the county records. I don't know who's behind it, or even why, for certain."

He snorted in annoyance and declared, "Them's not brass tacks, Ma'am. I can't do beans about vague feelings something may be stirring in the hen house. Name me one hen who's reported sighting one weasel!"

She said, "I can do better than that. It was my husband, Bob, who first noticed his county directory didn't completely agree with the last voter registration. I don't mean just the few names of folk who'd died but hadn't been removed from the voting lists yet. Bob said that always happened."

Longarm nodded casually. "Always will, as long as folk die right up to the day before an election. No harm done unless someone votes in their place before their name can be left out of more up-to-date listings."

He smiled thinly and added, "It's surprising how long it can take folk to notice they're dead and quit voting. But it tends to even out fair unless one party or the other suffers a plague, and I understand neither of the opposition slates have anyone running for sheriff against you next Tuesday. So what do you care if a few haunts vote for you, seeing they can hardly vote *against* you!"

She shook her head and said, "Not true. Jimmy Harper, you met him just last night, says there's talk of a write-in for Lewis Duncan. I asked, but both the Republican and Democrat election committees deny knowing anything about it. They say Lewis is registered as a Granger, the same as me."

Longarm thought, as he was paid to, before he decided, "I bet a write-in vote for a member of the same party as the one he or she might be running against could be contested easy. That's not saying a bunch of good old boys couldn't mark their ballots for a pal running as an *independent,* though. How many dead cowboys might old Lewis be able to call on?"

She smiled wanly and said, "It does sound silly in the cold light of day. But late at night I've gotten to fretting more about Bob and what he said about that last election, two years back."

Longarm frowned and demanded, "What could he have said? Neither he nor any other county official would have been running in an off-year election. That one two years ago was for the U.S. Congress and your territorial legislature, right?"

She nodded and said, "That's what they told Bob when he brought it up at a county board meeting. Supervisor

118

Burnett said he'd have Miss Chambrun run a name-by-name comparison of each and every listing and make certain everything was tidy by this fall."

Longarm asked if Miss Chambrun was that little gray fuzz-ball and learned they were talking about another gal entire who'd been hired on as county clerk after graduating from some she-male business school back East. The one who was serving as county sheriff continued, "Maybe she did. Nobody seems to know for certain. She quit without notice shortly after Bob was murdered. We have the original county directory as updated, they say, to this summer. I've a copy of that in my desk, of course, along with more recent transcriptions of the voting lists, according to three election committees. They don't begin to match up."

Longarm pursed his lips and decided, "Of course they don't. Lists of Democrats, Grangers, independents and Republicans ain't supposed to carry the same names. When you say transcriptions can I take it you mean you had someone copy the originals, with a court order, I hope?"

She dimpled up at him to demurely reply, "Don't be silly. I had some of my deputies investigate discreetly, after hours, when nobody was watching."

He heaved a great sigh and told her, "Such evidence ain't worth warm spit in court unless someone wants to charge you and your kid deputies with criminal trespass. But seeing you have the evidence on hand I'd best have a look at it. It might at least offer some hints as to what we're talking about!"

She popped back to her feet, saying all the records, for all they were worth, were in that big desk down below. So that was where they both went, putting on their Stetsons as they went down the harshly sunlit stairs.

As she led him around to the front entrance Matt said she'd shown the transcripts to others and that he was the first one who'd told her she'd done wrong.

To which he could only reply, "Takes a lawman to know all the laws, I reckon. Who'd you show 'em to, Miss Matt?"

She answered, "Beside my own deputies and members of our Granger election committee? Old Frank Flint at the

Monitor, for one. I thought he'd be anxious to print the story on his front page. But he acted as if he took me for a Nervous Nelly."

Longarm nodded and said, "He likely did. You never offered him no front page story, nor even a back page story, Miss Matt. Can't you get it through your pretty head that you can't just charge a person or persons unknown with being up to something you don't savvy? You can't just run a hobo in for singing a song you've never heard before across the way from that hen house I mentioned."

She said lots of peace officers might. But he insisted, "Two wrongs don't make a right and any lawyer worth his salt is going to get that melodious hobo off unless someone's missing one danged chicken."

By this time they were inside and young Jimmy Harper rose from where he'd been seated behind that big desk. When Matt asked him for those records in the left hand bottom drawer he bent over for 'em willingly enough. Then he searched all the other drawers, one by one, only to confess in a puzzled tone, "They don't seem to be here, Ma'am. Yet I know they were in that very drawer you just mentioned, just last night!"

Longarm was ahead of the she-sheriff as she turned to him and gasped, "Oh, Custis! What if that was what they were really after last night?"

To which he could only reply, "I'm sure they must have been, and to tell the truth I'm starting to feel a mite left out. But at least I'm more sure of *you,* now, Nervous Nelly."

So Longarm never got to peek into that picnic hamper or under that riding habit that afternoon. He and the she-sheriff wound up at a full board meeting with Supervisor Burnett and other county officials down to that little fuzzy gal, taking notes down to one end of the long trestle table on the step-up dais at one end of the Grange hall they borrowed for such occasions.

Matt confided they'd be holding the elections there, come Tuesday, followed by a victory ball, come Saturday, for whoever might win.

120

Old T. B. Burnett seemed to take Matt Flanders's charges in the spirit they seemed meant. It was the district attorney, backed up by a prune-faced justice of the peace, who commenced to give her what for for cribbing public records on the sly without a warrant.

Supervisor Burnett banged his gavel to shush them and chided, "Aw, come on, Dave. Public records are by definition public and I for one have felt ever-free to poke about in the files all I needed to when I had something I wanted to look up."

The district attorney said, "That's a horse of another color, T. B. You're talking about your own office files and a county directory we had Frank Flint print up for anybody with two bits to spare. Sending sneaks into the various campaign headquarters, after hours, to paw through party papers was unconstitutional!"

There was no telling how long they'd have bickered on about it if Longarm hadn't banged the table from his side and announced, "As the senior federal peace officer present I stand ready, willing and able to arrest anyone here on any federal charge related to the constitution of these United States, provided we see some due process, here."

The somewhat older and way fatter district attorney gasped, puffed up like a horny toad fixing to spit blood out its eyes, and demanded, "Are you trying to lecture me on the law, young sir?"

Longarm smiled, not unkindly, and replied, "Somebody ought to, no offense. We all do lots of things we mayhaps shouldn't ought to. Lord only knows what others might have been up to in that same dark as Miss Matt's boys took notes by candle glow, not damaging a speck of anyone's property. But to make a charge of mopery or even trespass stick you got to charge, try and *convict*. So for openers I'd like to hear whether any offended party committee would like to have me arrest any particular body on any particular charge, commencing with what harm was done and, oh, yeah, I'll need any records copied down and then stolen to present as evidence to the nearest federal court as would like to try the case."

121

There came a long moment of awkward silence. Then T. B. banged for attention on his own side of the table and said, "There you go, boys. No harm done and no dirty linen washed in public, right?"

An old gray gent who looked as if he'd been out here since the Shining Times and hadn't been slickered too often since, cleared his scrawny old throat to declare, "Strike that from the record, Miss Penny, and let's back up and start over right here."

Matt Flanders confided in a whisper to Longarm that the crusty old coot served as justice of the peace in an outlying township when he wasn't running the Republican election committee here in the county seat pro tem. They called him Judge Blake, even though "Judge" was only honorary for a country J.P.

The old man said, "My party, for one, stands ready to open its books to any interested party at any time and I didn't cotton to that snide remark about dirty linen at all, T. B."

Before the county supervisor could reply another older man chimed in, "Ditto for us Democrats, you red rag waving socializer! There'd be no point at all in registering voters by name if each and every party kept its list a deep dark secret!"

T. B. laughed easily and banged harder, declaring, "If you'd all simmer down I was just about to move we set aside the way Sheriff Flanders might have come by such records of her own and consider what we ought to do about 'em being stolen."

The little mousy gal taking down the minutes of the meeting raised her pencil for attention and when she got some squeaked, "Nothing is really missing. Nothing I can't get back for you within plenty of time before the election, I mean. I have my own copy of the county directory. Sheriff Flanders is only missing transcribed copies she ordered her deputies to make. The originals should be right where they belong and . . ."

"Then what are we wasting all this time over?" yelled a bearded wonder seated down at the other end in battered Texas hat and greasy sheepskin jacket. Longarm could see right off he was rich as well as cow. It was the kids just signing on to ride drag who sprang for all the rattlesnake hatbands and woolly chaps.

T. B. looked pained and explained, "We knew all along we still had all the county residents listed, along with how many of 'em get to vote next Tuesday, Mr. Logan. What you and Miss Penny seem to be missing is that the rascals who shot up the jail and run off with all those transcribed copies have 'em as well!"

The old stockman grumbled, "What of it? I've told ever'one who'd like to know I've always voted Democrat and always will. Don't care what Jeff Davis done down Montgomery way that time. Lincoln had his own faults, you know. Him and his dad-blamed homestead act sending Swedes and worse out here to fence the land just as we'd about cleared off the infernal Shoshone! What difference do it make, come Tuesday, if some sneak knows how all of us are registered? The *ballots* are still secret, ain't they?"

The old J.P. said, "Within reason. The purpose of having voters declare their affiliation and intent to vote before you let 'em do so is to hold crookery down to a roar. In times and places where elections ain't conducted as formal there's this inclination to stuff the ballot boxes with way more ballots than the true population figures call for, with the party with the most paper, and gall, inclined to claim the prizes."

T. B. swore—under his breath because of the ladies present—and hit the table in front of him a good lick before he yelled, "For land's sake can we knock off this civics lesson and hear some motions as to what's to be *done*? I move we have Sheriff Flanders, here, handle the break-in as any other breach of the peace and simply see if she and her boys can figure out who done it."

"She gets to arrest 'em when she does, don't she?" asked old Logan.

T. B. snorted and replied, "Well of course she gets to arrest 'em. They tried to kill Long, there, while they were robbing her desk! Are there any other motions?"

Longarm said, "Yep. I move Miss Penny, there, let's me have my own copy of her . . ."

123

"You ain't a member of this county council!" T. B. cut in, adding, "Even if you were you'd be asking too much. Miss Penny has better things to do on county time than check and double-check records that have already been double-checked and ain't been stolen!"

The little mousy gal demurely said, "Oh, I don't mind, and I can do it over the weekend, on my own time."

Longarm said, "I hadn't finished. I never meant to ask your county clerk's office for more paper than I'd like to stuff my saddlebags with. Sheriff Flanders tells me her late husband had mentioned some *discrepancies* betwixt the possibly out-of-date county directory and the voter registration and election back."

T. B. nodded but said, "We talked about that long before he was, ah, taken from us. Had it out with Frank Flint and you'll find the directory he ran off for us more recent is more up-to-date. As for Miss Penny rewriting every blamed name for you in longhand when you can have the fool directory *free . . .*"

"That ain't what I'm asking." Longarm cut in, swearing some under his own breath before adding, "All I'd like to ask Miss Penny here to do for me, if only you'd let me, is to jot down the name or names of anyone registered to vote for anyone, this Tuesday, whose name might not appear in the county directory."

Miss Penny smiled at him, it was some improvement, and told all of them how easy that would be, adding, "All I have to do is run down each page with a copy of the printed directory on hand. There are fewer than fifteen hundred registered voters all told and it sounds like fun!"

"Speak for yourself," murmured Matt Flanders under her breath, adding, "Poor little drab," as everyone else agreed and T. B. declared the next order of business to be that proposed timber truss spanning Poison Creek.

Matt Flanders nudged Longarm and suggested they got out of there before they found that interesting. As they rose to leave, the fuzzy little gal called out to ask Longarm when he might be calling on her for those figures. He said it was up to her. She suggested Sunday, after church. When he said that sounded fine, as long as her office was open on the sabbath, she told him not to be silly and that everyone knew where she lived.

As Longarm and the she-sheriff moved on that one laughed and said, "I'd better keep an eye on you and our Miss Penelope Nelson. I think she has *her* eye on *you*, Custis!"

He laughed incredulously and replied, "That poor old maid? Surely you jest, Ma'am. You just heard her say she wanted to meet me after church."

Matt sighed and said, "Praying doesn't really help that much when a woman's really lonely, and who's to say what any of us might be praying for? Would you like to go for that ride out to Medicine Skull Rise now, Custis?"

He glanced up at the sky as they were leaving the hall. He said, "Well, it ain't too late in the *day* for a picnic, albeit it's a tad late in the fall and the wind's been shifting north."

She laughed and said it wasn't that far. So he said he was game and he meant it. But when they got back to her office it was only to learn some things just weren't meant to be, no matter what anyone might agree to.

Chapter 15

There were fourteen Indian ponies and almost as many Indians lined up out front of the sheriff's department. Others must have been watching from inside. For three came out, along with two white deputies, as Longarm and the she-sheriff approached.

The Indians were bundled against the sunny but crisp weather in a mishmash of buckskins, trading post duds and army hand-me-downs. They looked more Mex that your generally taller horse Indians of the northern grasslands. So Longarm figured them for Shoshone. They looked more Mex for the simple reason that the Aztec, Yaqui, Pima, Chihuahua and such had been linguistic and likely blood kin to the Shoshone, Bannock, Paiute and such who'd orginated in the Great Basin betwixt the Sierra Nevadas and the Rockies in a younger and greener world.

The obvious leader of this bunch seemed a mere kid, chosen for a better handle on English. The squirt wore a visored Army forage cap over long braided hair and a bulky blue Army greatcoat over fringed leggings and beaded moccasins. Dressed more sensible, the kid might have passed for a more-Spanish-than-Mestizo pretty boy. So Longarm had the sort of snooty priss down as likely a Metis or Canadian breed. Some said they were the most treacherous kind.

Longarm had met some decent Metis, though. So he howdied everyone there as friendly as he waited to see if he'd guessed right about the one in charge of whatever this might be.

The kid in the forage cap proved him right by saying, "You can call me Colorado if my true name, Lee Kollorow, sits awkward on your saltu tongue. The old ones sent me and these young men to escort you into a big council they've called to decide on peace or war, if you'd be willing to come. I hope you'll say no. My friends and me are all for war. But some of the old ones say they want to hear what Saltu Ka Saltu has to say for his own people, first."

Matilda Flanders clutched Longarm's sleeve to softly warn, "Be careful, Custis. It sounds like a trap, to me."

Longarm shrugged and said for all to hear, "If it is, and I don't get out of it alive, we'll say no more about it, Ma'am. But it's been my experience my Ho-speaking brothers fight like men. I've never heard of 'em extending a formal invite to a council with anyone they were out to back-stab."

He got out a single cheroot and thumbnailed a match to light it with as he continued, "My brothers have caught me at a bad time to ride so far with them, though. I hadn't heard about any trouble between Great Father and his Shoshone children. I was sent here to make sure none of these saltu cheat when they decide on who they want to lead them in just a few days."

Kollorow said, "I just said I'd rather you refused to come with us. But I'd be speaking as straight as you people like to if I didn't tell you my elders are meeting, along with their adopted Arapaho children, just this side of the Wind River, maybe twenty-five of your miles from here. If we left now you could attend the council tonight, sleep over, and get back here in time to get good and drunk the night before you people like to visit the kiva of your big kachina, Jesus."

Longarm smiled dryly and replied, "I can see you didn't pick up much religious instruction along with your English from the saltu side of your family, Lee. What might you be able to tell me about the trouble brewing betwixt Saltu and Ho? I just got here."

The good-looking but sullen-faced breed said, "Maybe I got more birchings for Kachina Jesus and his mamma from my mamma than I really needed to see how silly those teachings are. Didn't Jesus tell all you saltu to follow those ten teachings of Kachina Moses, and wasn't there something in them about not *lying,* even to poor fucking diggers?"

Longarm warned, "Watch it, old son. Ladies present and if you aim to get picky it was the Canaanites old Moses and his boys went after for reasons that have ever escaped me. There was nothing about Shoshone in the good book you seem so fond of citing."

Kollorow said something sarcastic in Ho to the others. Some chuckled but none of them smiled friendly at Longarm as their leader continued in English, "I remember that part about your big Saltu Kachina promising the land of Canaan to outsiders the Canaanites had never done bad things to. I just *told* you what I think of your forked-tongue ways. Some of my father's people seem to think you people are somehow going to change. They think just because they have it in writing, in both tongues, that the lands you set aside for the Washakie Shoshone, the little part of this land that was once all Ho, might be their little bit of land for as long as the waters shall run and the grass shall grow."

Longarm saw the Shoshone patriot was getting all wound up to talk as dumb as some of his own kind. So he cut in, not unkindly, "I'll bet you a month's pay you can't show me one fool treaty signed by anyone with any connection with any U.S. Government, past or present, saying anything at all about waters running or grass growing."

It was Matt Flanders who looked surprised and said she'd read some place about George Washington in the flesh signing some such treaty with some tribe or other back east.

Lee Kollorow nodded and said, "Listen to her. She's not as dumb as you, after all, Saltu Ka Saltu!"

Longarm chuckled and said, "I've won many a bar bet, for such a dumb cuss. George Washington never promised anything to any Indians for the simple reason he just plain didn't like any of the nations he'd fought and didn't feel he needed to promise a thing to friendlies, such as the Stockbridge Algonquins who'd enlisted in his Continental

Army and acted natural, to his way of thinking."

"Maybe it was someone else, then," the she-sheriff decided.

Longarm shook his head and said, "You ought to read some legal documents instead of trusting to the words of reporters who have the young George Washington cutting down cherry trees or Paul Revere being the one who carried that warning to Concord. Treaties are drawn up in lawyer talk by lawyers, not poets. Most I've read have read so dry and dusty it's small wonder so many folk, on both sides, have paid no mind to more than one."

Lee Kollorow snapped, "Hear me! We who speak Ho have never broken our word to anyone, never!"

Longarm shrugged and said, "I reckon them saltu women at the White River Agency got what was coming to 'em from them Ho they'd been feeding and clothing so recent. But I never said our side has never broken a treaty. Lawyer talk was invented to get around."

He tried handing the cheroot he'd just lit to Lee Kollorow as he continued, "Be that as it may, I ride for the current government and you boys know I'm willing to own up to fighting Shoshone back in '78. So I doubt they'd keep it a secret from me if they were planning to evict so many of you little red rascals from your Wind River Reserve."

The young breed ignored the offering of tobacco to sniff and reply, "Not all of it. Only *half* of it, *this* time. Another saltu ka saltu who speaks Ho better than you has told the old ones the Great Father means to take all the buffalo hunting grounds on this side of the Wind River for his own longhorn cattle. He is only waiting until after this election rite you mentioned before."

Longarm whistled and stuck the cheroot back in his own teeth, seeing Lee Kollorow wanted to act so rude, before he decided, "I'd best ride west with you boys and assure some doubtless worried folk. This other helpful stranger you've cited has to be a troublemaker with an axe of his own to grind, Lee. You have my word as one man to another that I've heard nothing about such a barefaced land grab."

Matt Flanders protested, "What about the election, Custis?"

129

To which he could only reply, "You'll play hell *holding* one in the middle of an Indian rising and you just heard this boy say I can make it back by Saturday night."

The Shoshone elders had sent along a saddled paint pony for Saltu Ka Saltu. But Longarm still insisted they all drop by the nearby livery stable, where he picked up his thigh-length sheepskin jacket, in case it got even brisker, and his Winchester saddle gun, just in case.

Lee Kollorow waited until they were leaving town, out on point with the others trailing, before dryly saying, "I think it is going to get colder, too. But do you really think that rifle will make any difference if I've been speaking with a forked tongue?"

Longarm shrugged and replied, "Not to *me,* in the end, but she'll be throwing sixteen rounds as I go down. So that ought to make some difference in the final score."

Kollorow chuckled and said, "It's too bad they asked us to bring you in alive. I think it would be a good fight. I have been thinking about what you said about what happened down at the White Springs Agency, not so long ago. It is true our Ute brothers speak Ho. But Quinkent and his followers had good reasons to do bad things to that B.I.A. agent who attacked them for no reason, none!"

Longarm lit another cheroot to give himself time to think back on the affair before he flatly replied, "Bullshit. A lot of folk, red and white, including some I know in the B.I.A. have told me Agent Meeker, Nathan C., was an incompetent political hack who'd failed as a newspaper man and real estate developer before he'd tried civilizing Indians with utopian notions about amber waves of grain in the Rocky Mountains."

Kollorow said, "He told his own people to plow under the best winter pasture for a day's ride. He did this in the moon of falling leaves, just before the soil was about to freeze all the way down to the bedrock. The Utes asked Agent Meeker not to do this. They told him there was flatter ground, not as good grazing, if he wanted to act silly. Meeker called them bad names. When they called him a fool he called them bad Indians and sent for the soldiers."

Longarm nodded grimly but said, "I just allowed Nate Meeker was a fool. It wasn't bright to open fire on that cavalry column sent to look into the matter, neither."

"The Utes say the soldiers fired first." Lee Kollorow objected.

To which Longarm replied as surely, "Soldiers always fire first when their leader's dismounted to move forward afoot, waving his hat for a parley. Is it this cheap tobacco or do I taste snow in the air this afternoon?"

Lee Kollorow sniffed and said, "I have been wondering how long it would take a saltu to notice. If we have very good medicine today we may make the council fires along the tree-sheltered river before the blizzard. If it catches us out here in the open we can only press on until we get to the river, or until the snow gets too deep."

You didn't have to stand in the stirrups to see far under the big skies of Wyoming Territory. So Longarm glared back at the gathering gray fury to the north northeast with his cheroot gripped between his bared teeth as he observed, "We're one hell of a heap closer to Medicine Skull than the Wind River and I wouldn't bet on making her back to town before the first flakes hit. Do you know of any fairly deep and well-timbered draws we might be able to follow west if we're dumb enough to press on with a blue norther fixing to hit?"

His guide looked undecided, then pointed off to their right to say, uncertainly, "That way. But even if I was willing to shelter in such a place these others who ride with us would be afraid."

Longarm naturally asked how come. The young breed explained, "The draw begins as a gully down the west side of the rise the forgotten ones made a medicine ring on. Later Cheyenne put a medicine skull on a rock pile, there. We heard the skull is gone and that now young saltu fuck girls there and litter the grass between the rocks of the medicine ring with broken glass and those rubber things you people fuck with."

Longarm didn't reply as he digested the interesting afternoon ride he seemed to have just missed. Kollorow continued, "My saltu mother was not as afraid of ghosts as the rest of my people, either. That gully turns into an ever deeper draw as it winds west toward the Wind River. There are trees, big trees, but those Cheyenne still hunted this far west and fought us for the country you see all around us right now."

Longarm nodded and asked, "Are we talking about bad fights in that otherwise handy draw, Lee?"

The young breed repressed a shudder and said, "Worse than bad fights. Bad medicine. I was not there. It was so long ago all but a few very old ones were told about it by their own elders. They say it was at the time the stars fell down and people were falling down, too, all over."

Longarm nodded and said, "I've read about the meteor showers and smallpox plague of the thirties. Wiped the Mandan out entire and played hob with most of the nations out this way. Are you saying a heap of your folk died along that wooded draw, Lee?"

His guide snorted in disdain and demanded, "Who would be afraid of *friendly* dead? Didn't you just hear me say we were fighting *Cheyenne* for this country? They say it was about this time of the year. Those Cheyenne had taken many of our ponies, many of our girls, and even some of our hair. So clever Shoshone war chiefs gathered a really big war band, later in the year than usual, to hit the Cheyenne as they were going into winter camp."

Longarm nodded and said, "Cheyenne I know say you Ho speakers were their favorite enemies, too. There was way more brag in lifting the hair and cutting the fingers off a Shoshone, Bannock or Ute than say a Pawnee or Ree."

The breed snorted in disgust and said, "There's no honor at all in killing a *Ree*. Ree smack their lips when they smell the shit of real men and count coup when they rape their sisters. Ree don't have to rape their own mothers and . . . We were talking about Cheyenne. Cheyenne are worth having as enemies, most of the time. But over in that wooded draw our young men struck one cold gray dawn to find all their good enemies dead. All. Men, women, children. Some outside but most inside their lodges, as if they'd gone to sleep and never got up the next day. But they were stinking, stinking, as if they had been dead even longer than they could have been."

Longarm nodded soberly and said, "I've smelled a fever ward or more in my time. But if even a whole Cheyenne village died of smallpox over forty years ago, Lee, how much could be left of any grim remains at this late date?"

The Shoshone breed repressed a shudder and replied, "I don't know, I've never been there. Nobody with any respect for medicine goes there. Cheyenne are mean enough when they're *alive*!"

Longarm said he'd heard as much as they rode on 'neath an ever-darkening sky. He'd figured on them reaching that council along the river just in time for supper. Now he was hoping to just reach it. He knew they'd never see any sunset no matter when it got really dark on such a gray wool day. He wasn't sure just how late in the day it might be, right now. It was tougher to judge time with no sun up there to go by. His pocket watch said it was going on two-thirty. But he wasn't certain when they'd left Medicine Skull. He was sorely tempted to turn back, whether his armed escort liked it or not. For there was just no way they were going to make the fifteen or more miles ahead of them before the storm hit, unless they got a damned move on.

He said as much, suggesting, "It ought to be mostly downhill from here to the Wind River, Lee. At a lope, with the ponies this cool, we ought to be able to make her in an hour or so."

His guide glanced up at the skudding clouds as if for further guidance before yelling loud in Ho and picking up the pace. Longarm heeled his own mount from a slow trot to an easy lope and, if nothing else, it felt more comfortable to him and probably the paint under him. For ponies felt more frisky when it was cold and tended to head for home way faster than they cottoned to heading the other way.

But they hadn't loped more than a few furlongs when the wind picked up of a sudden to try blowing them off the rise they were topping. Failing that, it peppered their faces good with snowflakes frozen dry as the brake sand of a locomotive.

It felt better down in the next grassy draw but of course they knew they had to ride up and over, through more of the same, to get anywhere worth mentioning. As the wind

133

howled wolfishly just above them Longarm yelled, "No shit, we'd best make for that deeper-timbered draw before we get our balls froze off and blown away!"

Lee Kollorow insisted on beelining on. So they tried, even though topping the next rise hurt worse, and the shallow draw beyond had already accumulated a good inch of snow.

Longarm knew it figured to get worse before it got better. He'd been caught in the open by early blizzards before. He said so, next time he could make himself heard above the howling winds, adding, "No shit, kid. If you're afraid of long dead folk the least we can try is turning our backs to this wind in as low a spot as we can manage."

Then he saw nobody seemed to be listening to him. So he could only swear and ride on after the stubborn breed with the shifting winds snow-blasting them most everywhere but their left sides—and their right sides as naturally plastered white and rapidly turning numb.

Then, moving over another rise with the blizzard blinding him and his mount, he wound up falling, pony and all, and only saved himself from getting rolled by swinging out of his saddle across the belly and between the thrashing legs of the equally-startled paint.

Longarm landed on his right side and almost on top of young Kollorow in the lee of the breed's own roan. So he naturally asked how come.

The kid replied in a dazed tone, "I'm not sure. He just seemed to drop out from under me. Is that him, fussing so?"

Longarm rolled to his hands and knees for a better look at the roan in the almost hopeless visibility. Then he swore, drew his .44-40 and placed the muzzle against the depression just over the injured mount's widely rolling right eye, muttering "prairie dog hole" before he pulled the trigger.

That inspired the paint he'd been riding to struggle to its own sounder legs and light out, downwind, as Longarm called it awful names but didn't try running after it through a gale-force blizzard. It hurt so much, just standing there, he hunkered back down behind the dead roan with its rider to confide, "We're up shit creek and if you don't have a paddle I sure hope you've got a bedroll, here, kid."

The young breed replied, "Of course I have a bedroll. But I'm not sure I want to go to bed with you and can't we manage a fire in the lee of poor old Tsen Wa Ouray?"

Longarm grimaced and replied, "With what? Even if we could get oil-soaked tinder and a cord of pitch pine right now we'd never be able to *light* it in this wind. Your pals have ridden on. If any of 'em miss us and turn back I don't see how they'll find us in this howling blue norther. But early November blizzards tend to blow over as sudden as they sprung up. So let's see what we can do to stay alive 'til this one gets tired of trying to kill us."

He propped himself up on one elbow, nearly losing his hat, and groped upwind for the bedroll lashed to the breed's old army saddle, saying, "I could tell you a tale about saving myself and two saltu ladies in a storm worse than this one. But I wouldn't want you to get the notion I was suggesting we bundle up *that* friendly. No offense, but you just ain't my type."

Lee Kollorow hesitated before replying, thoughtfully, "What's wrong with me? I'd never want to get that friendly with you, as a rule. But I know what you mean about warming up a bedroll and it's going to get a lot colder before this storm blows itself out!"

Longarm went on unlashing the bedroll anyway. He knew that Indians tended to take a much more tolerant, or maybe practical, attitude toward the sins of Sodom. The Lakota, despite their reputation as fighting men, had a sort of sissy society to compliment and even pleasure the warrior societies. They held a boy who grew up with girlish feelings to be no more unusual than, say, a kid who shot left-handed or busted out in a rash from eating berries.

Thinking of a she-sheriff who shot left-handed didn't ease Longarm's mind about bedding down with anyone as he unrolled the young breed's bedding in the lee of the dead pony. Thanks to the way the wind was sweeping over them the snow was already getting deep on their side. They knew there'd be less snow and a lot more wind on the far side. Longarm said, "Well, I got to admit this is going to be a mite snug. On the other hand, if we both get in and let the dry snow cover us it'll surely have freezing to death beat."

Suiting actions to his words Longarm opened the end closer to the belly of the dead roan to slide in, boots first, without even removing his hat. "I'll get in and then we'll see if you can shoehorn your smaller frame in with mine."

Lee Kollorow did so, but removed that bulky greatcoat first and draped it atop the already snow-frosted canvas and the Longarm-stuffed blankets before sliding in, all softer and warmer buckskin, to say with a sigh, "You will be gentle, after I've had time to warm up to the thought of letting you, right?"

Longarm snorted in mingled surprise and disgust, with both of them, as he tried to shift away from the disturbingly inviting warmth of his unplanned on bedfellow. Then he growled, "Don't talk like an asshole. Even if I wanted to get at your asshole right now I don't see how I could."

The much-smaller breed chuckled, sort of dirty, and suggested, "It might help if you took off that gun belt and do we really need that bulky jacket you have on, under all these covers?"

Longarm swore softly and replied, "Never mind what I got on, old son. And be advised I'm likely to react hasty if anyone goes to feeling me up for weapons or anything else when I'm starting to doze off!"

Lee Kollorow murmured, "Old *son?* Kachina Jesus, have you been thinking I was a *boy* all this time?"

Longarm was too thundergasted to reply until the kid grabbed one of his hands. Then he said, "You'd better not be!" as he grasped where his hand was being guided, gently but firmly.

Then he laughed and said, "Well, I'll be a dumb son of a bitch!" as she placed his palm against a firm young breast, saying, "I know. But let's fuck anyway. I'm really starting to feel that wind out there, now!"

So they did and it was better the second time, after they'd warmed up the bedroll enough to shuck everything and do it right. She kissed whiter than Marie had. Longarm didn't care to know who might have taught her. A gal with the

136

features of a sixteen-year-old boy had to be somewhat older and he was glad her hair smelled faintly of naptha soap. Her body felt firm and young enough as well as reasonably clean. Riding a lot, astride, did wonders for any woman's thighs, hips and waistline. That was doubtless why so many Victorian spoilsports were so dead set against gals riding with their knees spread natural, lest they or any of their pals wind up enjoying the results.

Lee said she enjoyed keeping warm with him that way but warned him not to tell any of her Shoshone pals she'd been this friendly with a fucking saltu. He didn't ask why. She'd already told him she was a paid-up member of the war party.

He could only hope, as they tried yet another position under the snow-covered canvas and the wolf winds howled for their blood, he could talk her people out of another war. For she said that as a translator she'd be out in front a lot and he knew how the U.S. Cav felt about parleys with hostiles since old Major Thornburgh had been shot out from under that truce flag at Milk River.

It would likely be best for all concerned if he could head off such confrontations before anyone he admired could wind up trying to stop a field artillery round with her pretty face.

Chapter 16

The blizzard had blown itself out before morning. So a bright sun rose in a cloudless sky of cobalt blue to grin into the teeth of yet another kind of chinook.

The *chinook* wind, or "snow burner," had nothing to do with the lingo that went by the same name, save that both originated west of the Continental Divide. As a wind, the chinook dropped all its rain or snow on the far slopes and tore down the eastern slopes much dryer and warmer as it got denser, sinking ever lower, until it could blow shirtsleeve-warm in the middle of winter.

Folk died of pneumonia a lot in your average Wyoming winter, which was seldom average from one day to the next.

Lee toted her bedding and saddle bags, afoot, as Longarm trudged along beside her with her saddle. They tried to avoid the low places as they made their weary way across a big paint-pony hide of leftover snow and soggy brown shortgrass. Longarm's socks were still squishing in his stovepipe boots and Lee had removed her beaded moccasins to walk bare of foot and blue of toe by the time some of her Shoshone kin found them out in the middle of all that thaw.

They'd even recovered Longarm's Winchester, bless them, albeit, they explained, with Lee translating, they'd found that paint frozen to death between where it had run off from and where it might have thought it was running, poor brute.

They'd naturally set out to find Longarm and the missing breed gal with fresh mounts. So it was well before noon when they all rode into conditions as uncertain as Custer's scouts might have reported at another time and place. A haze of woodsmoke hung amid the bare gray branches of cottonwood and willow along the Wind River. Most Horse Indians had given up tipi rings for closely related reasons to the fact that most cavalry officers preferred to open fire at dawn and parley later with any chastened survivors. So a tipi here and another there, scattered among the groves of cottonwood and tangles of willow, were all you saw as you moved in on a mighty vague number of Indians.

Longarm could tell some of them had to be Arapaho. Some said Arapaho had invented the tipi. Others said it was a notion early wanderers had brought all the way from the hills and plains of Siberia. In either case Arapaho tipis stood higher and fancier than most, with their hide or canvas covers speckled or striped in brighter colors. Arapaho favored green as much as Lakota admired red.

Most of the tipis they passed were naturally the more solidly planted and stolidly decorated lodges Shoshone preferred. There were two common ways to put up a tipi. Arapaho women, like their Cheyenne cousins, erected a three pole tripod and then leaned lots of other poles against that in a circle. The Shoshone, like Comanche, Utes and other distant kin, started with *four* poles, forming a roomier square at ground level. Both sides claimed their design was best in a windstorm. Longarm felt it depended more on the skills of the individual builder and to prove this he'd noticed others who'd come later to the High Plains had taken construction tips from both Ho and Algonquin-speaking teachers without regard to their own background.

Thus the Teton Lakota or so-called Western Sioux followed the three-pole Arapaho style, while their Absaroka, Hidasta and Omaha cousins, along with Algonquin-speaking Siksika or Blackfoot favored the squatter Shoshone style.

Lee Kollorow reined in near a particularly squat tipi decorated mostly with smoke stains and indicated he ought to dismount as well. So he did and when another rider led their ponies off somewhere he felt just as glad he'd hung on to his Winchester, this time.

He followed the pretty breed inside, ducking low through the round opening poked through the south sunny side. As his eyes adjusted to the gloom inside he was mildly surprised to see they were alone in what seemed more a field etapé or storage tent than a dwelling. He noticed more bedding on the far side of the piled bales and boxes as Lee told him, "This is the lodge we've been letting that other saltu ka saltu use. I thought you would want to talk to him before you spoke to the old ones. I like you, a little, and I didn't want you to make a fool of yourself."

Longarm smiled down at her to reply, "I like you a little, too, and I'd be proud to hear what this other white boy has to say about a land grab. For unless he's full of it, I ought to get to arrest some damned body around here. Guess who I get to arrest if he's only been out to incite a riot, federal."

She said, "They told me he was only here a few minutes ago. You can see he hasn't taken away the trade goods he brought to this big council. Maybe he's already joined the old ones in the council lodge. If I take you there, now, do you think you can hold your tongue until you know what's going on?"

He reached under his sheepskins thoughtfully as he told her he got paid to know what might be going on. Her eyes widened when she saw him opening his big pocket knife and grasped his full intent.

She said, "No! Stealing is only allowed from the lodge of an enemy and the trader who owns all this is under the protection of my nation!"

Longarm soothed, "I ain't out to steal toad squat, Honey. I'm only aiming to see what such a helpful cuss might be selling, seeing both you and the Arapaho should have picked up your cash allotments for this quarter. What's the name of this other saltu ka saltu, by the way?"

She said, "Something like Snake, in your language, I mean. Don't open that case, Custis!"

But he'd already pried up the end of one board, growling, "Snake seems too nice a word for the son of a bitch.

These reconditioned rifles are old Spencer repeaters, good enough to get our War Department excited as a wildcat with turpentine smeared under its tail, but not good enough to stand up to Gatling guns. That's what they'll bring in, along with field artillery, the moment they hear about another Shoshone rising with both sides packing repeaters!"

She grabbed his wrist and pleaded, "Don't make me call for help, Custis. You know I like you enough to fuck you but I can't let you steal Mister Snake's trade goods!"

He shook his head and hammered the loose board back in place with his free fist as he soothed, "I'm not about to try and sneak out of a camp this size in broad daylight with at least a gross of rifles and Lord knows how much ammunition. Let's go see this Mr. Snake and the rest of your damned fool friends!"

They tried. Lee wound him through the trees and tipis to a bigger one covered with antique buffalo hide and serious-looking medicine signs. But when she called in through the low entry and got some answers in rapid-fire Ho, she told Longarm, "Mr. Snake is not here, either. But they say they want to talk to you."

So Longarm ducked on in with the girl following to translate or perhaps to take part, for all he knew. Indians seemed to respect the she-male brain a heap for the wife-beating savages they were widely held to resemble.

Longarm had been to these councils or caucuses before, caucus being an Indian word the more familiar Republicans and Democrats had picked up from some otherwise-primitive Algonquins, so he knew the mostly older gents came and went throughout the day as the spirit or something stuck in the craw might move 'em. It was tougher to tell Shoshone from Arapaho in such dim light with everyone wearing winter trading-post duds. But the fact that Indians speaking different tongues were pissed off and in congress assembled was a blessing to an outsider fluent in neither lingo. Few Shoshone could talk Arapaho any better than Longarm, and vice versa, so the two nations of the Wind River Agency carried on most of their diplomacy in English, with the elders speaking for either nation getting plenty of practice. So Longarm didn't need a translator when one old moon-faced cuss with bullet-hole eyes nodded at him to say, "We are very cross with all you saltu, all! You are treating us the way you treated our Ute brothers to the south. They let you have half their hunting grounds, more than half, without a fight, when the Great Father said they would get to keep all the lands, all, west of the Shining Mountains. But the Great Father spoke with a forked tongue and now all the Utes have been forced to live on roots and rabbits in the dry sage country west of the Green River!"

A couple of others agreed. One asked, mildly, whether it was true saltu spoke to their mothers-in-law and even slept with cousins, like the abominable Ree.

Longarm waited until nobody was cussing him before he replied, as mildly, "It was your Ho-speaking Ute cousins who killed eight men and raped three women, including a little girl, at the White River Agency. It was smart of them to ambush that army column on the Milk River, too. In the end they got frog-marched all the way to Utah Territory and I reckon they do get to nibble jackrabbits along with their B.I.A. rations."

"Agent Meeker at White River was a bad man who oppressed Quinkent and his people!" wailed another old cuss, out of turn.

Longarm frowned severely and said, "I am still speaking. Saltu I know in the B.I.A. agree Nate Meeker was a fool who had no business trying to run an Indian agency. I heard about him plowing up good grazing in a vain attempt to grow corn at high altitude with winter coming on. I heard about him insulting Quinkent and them other Utes he didn't even try to understand. But they sure as hell never met him halfway and it's tough to convince anyone you're all that noble when you gun down oppressive carpenters, masons and such before you get around to raping little girls."

The old Shoshone with the mean eyes tried, "Quinkent and his young men were excited. The soldiers were coming to murder them all and take their last lands away."

Longarm shook his head and said, "Bullshit. It was another Ute band, led by Nicaagat, who fired on Major Thornburgh's column after they'd sent Lieutenant Cherry ahead on foot to parley."

The older man insisted, "They had to defend themselves. Meeker had sent for the soldiers, saying bad things about all the Utes!"

Longarm shrugged and said, "I just agreed there were damned fools on both sides. When it was all over twelve soldiers and eight civilians lay dead and I reckon you could count coup on the three raped and forty-three wounded. Then the army counted coup on around forty Utes, including some leaders they got to hang as renegades, and frog-marched all the other members of the White and Milk River bands off to Utah, as you said."

Three old Indians tried to cuss him at once. He hushed them with one of the few Ho cuss words he knew and insisted, "Meanwhile the smarter Utes to the south saved their own hides and their reserve by disavowing Quinkent and Nicaagat as damned fools, which they were, no matter how you slice it. I was down to the South Ute Agency on another case, a spell back. They ain't been bothering anyone and vice versa."

The old man who'd asked about white mothers-in-law snorted and complained, "The little strip of land you people left the Utes in Colorado is nothing, nothing, to what they held in the Shining Times!"

Longarm nodded gravely and replied, "It's still a heap more than the White or Milk River bands wound up with. Many a cattle combine would consider that two thousand square miles of guaranteed Indian land a mighty fine cow pasture. But I doubt any Ute would be dumb enough, at this late date, to give anyone an excuse to run them off it."

Old Bullet Eyes brushed imaginary flies away and said, "We never sent for you to talk about Ute troubles. We have our *own* troubles. A trader we know well, who speaks our tongue, says that as soon as that election is over in a few days the saltu over to the east are going to tell us to move all our people and belongings over that river just to the west. The B.I.A. agents and army officers at Fort Washakie say he speaks with a forked tongue and want us to tell them his name. We don't want to do that. If we decide to fight for these last lands we have been allowed to keep we will need guns, many guns, and a saltu ka saltu who knows where to get them for us."

Longarm whistled softly and said, "There ain't that many guns in this whole world, old son. Like I said, lots of old boys would just love to see you shiftless wards of the government shifted off all this prime range."

He was dying for a smoke. He knew what a social gaffe it would be to light up at a council without being invited to. He wet his dry teeth with his tongue and said, "I was sent to make sure that election you mentioned gets conducted straight. So I know who's running for what and you have my word nobody is going to have much to say about the Bureau of Indian Affairs no matter who wins next Tuesday."

The old man insisted, "Our other saltu ka saltu says cowmen on both sides want all the grass as far west as the mountains. Maybe farther."

Longarm nodded and said, "I'm sure they do. There are saltu in high places who'd be proud to sell it to them, cheap, if you boys gave them the excuse to run you off and declare it uninhabited federal range. So why don't you just simmer down and not give anyone any such excuse?"

An even older cuss, who'd been listening instead of preaching, up until then, croaked, "This young man speaks wise as Old Coyote. Haven't I been telling you children I was there when Custer came to take those white girls fools were holding in Motavato's camp along the Washita? None of us Arapaho wintering there had any captives. We still lost most of our ponies and many young men, many, when the Blue Sleeves came with red thoughts about a few girls some silly Cheyenne had been fucking."

Longarm nodded and said, "My Arapaho grandfather understands war the way my people wage it. This girl you sent to bring me here said you wanted me to speak straight. So hear this. Our General Sheridan says the only good Indian is a dead Indian. There are others, even army men like Wood and Wynkoop, who speak up for you when they can. If you go on the warpath or even threaten to go on the warpath, before or after that election, nobody will be able to speak up for you and your Mr. Snake won't be able to bring you enough guns to win because there just aren't that many guns and I have spoken!"

The old bullet-eyed cuss blinked his bullet eyes and almost smiled as he said, "Snake? We have no snake bringing news and guns to us. Our saltu ka saltu is called Blake, Judge Blake, didn't you know that?"

Longarm smiled thinly and murmured, "I know it *now.*"

Chapter 17

Longarm had said he'd likely make it back to Medicine Skull by Saturday night. But it wasn't easy. Aside from being a good ride, a heap of it uphill, the damned wind shifted some more, and while the sky remained clear, it got almost as cold as a banker's heart again.

Riding alone without superstitious Shoshone, he tried avoiding some of those sudden gusts from the north by ducking down into that deeper timbered draw Lee Kollorow had down as bad medicine. A strip of bare but wind-breaking branches one could follow a dozen miles or more had to be just what the medicine man had ordered.

Even the fresh buckskin the Indians had given him heaved a mighty sigh of relief when, once he'd found that draw, they found the air almost dead still and one hell of a lot warmer in the sun-dappled shade of the interlocking branches as they trotted east across sand spangled with clumps of dead weeds. A lot was tumble-weed but, down here out of the wind, it didn't seem to matter.

The pony didn't notice, being more inclined to go by sounds and smells than sight, when they came upon the meager traces of what had once been as strung out an encampment as the one they'd left earlier that day. Organic stuff wasn't preserved up this way as down to the south-west. Forty-odd years of mighty fickle weather had reduced the few tipi frames still standing to little more than sun-silvered tripods, with only the stouter foundation poles firmly in place. The bleached human bones scattered about had a few beads or buttons mingled with them to show they hadn't all died naked as well as untended. He didn't see any rusty guns or tools in passing. Indians could be practical as well as superstitious if they hadn't known a dead cuss well enough to be recognized in broad day by his haunt.

A mile or so on, the Indian pony he was riding shied at something in the trees ahead. Longarm steadied it and pressed on at a more cautious walk. When he spied the tree burials up in some cottonwoods ahead he swung wide, agreeing with his mount, "That does seem a stinky way to dispose of one's dead kin, Buck. But neither you nor me are Cheyenne."

As they passed the grim but sort of fancy bundles off to their left, he continued, "I'd say Cheyenne because Lee said nobody from *her* agency has been up this draw in living memory."

He sniffed hard and added, "Hasn't been any Cheyenne in these parts for a couple of summers, either, come to study on it. We'd best forget them poor cadavers lest some pest collect 'em for some museum, seeing they must be about stunk-out by now."

They followed the wooded draw east until the trees thinned out and the wind started getting at them some more. Then Longarm nodded and swung up to their right across open, wind-whipped shortgrass, saying, "We didn't want to go all the way to Medicine Skull Rise. Meanwhile the town and a warm stall for you lies just over the skyline I got you headed for, so why don't you *move* it, Buck?"

The buckskin did, to get them into the county seat pro tem just as the sunset was making the frozen grass all around a mockery of glowing coals. Longarm was still considering how he meant to deal with Judge Blake as he dismounted stiffly in front of the livery. He went through the motions of putting a pony away whilst he thought about more important matters.

The old mountain man cum small-time politico cum dangerous pain in the ass was almost surely going to cite his first amendment rights the moment anyone accused him of speaking freely to those Indians. As even a self-taught J. P., he'd know free speech included the right to opine his fellow whites might covet all that swell grazing, or even timber and mineral rights west of the Wind River. Longarm knew this to be the simple truth. Just as he knew that if the Shoshone hadn't lost at least half of their present reserve by the turn of the century it would only be because his own kind was losing its grip.

He'd meant it when he'd promised them that morning that the coming election meant nothing to them, one way or the other. He'd felt fairly safe in assuring them they'd probably keep most of their land as long as old Carl Schurz got to run the B.I.A. But did that mean old Blake hadn't had the right to tell his Indian pals they were likely to get screwed some more sooner or later? It wasn't as if such screwings had never happened before and, right, how many federal prosecutors wanted to try a kindly old country J. P. for worrying about noble savages?

A lot of reporters had written a lot of things about running guns to Indians. A lot of army officers and their congressmen had said it was wrong and that there should have been a law. But there wasn't. It was still *whiskey* you weren't allowed to sell to anyone listed by the B.I.A. as a ward of the Government.

Indians listed as friendlies were issued hunting rifles and ammo by their Indian agents. So the most serious things old Blake could be charged with would be high-pressure sales tactics without a reservation peddler's license.

Parting friendly with the colored hostler, Longarm headed over to the she-sheriff's place, muttering half aloud, "Let's just give a snake enough rope and see what he does with it. He might not know how much we know and even a country J. P. knows enough about the law to hiss for some habeas corpus, and get it, unless we can get more on him than we have."

Matt Flanders answered his knock at the head of those outside stairs and hauled him in out of the nip, saying, "Thank heavens, I was starting to worry about you, too!

Where were you when that freak blizzard hit us yesterday afternoon?"

He shrugged and murmured something about sheltering with friendly Indians as she led him back to her kitchen and sat him at one end of her table, saying, "I just ate supper but it'll only take me a minute to rustle something up for you. Take off that coat, it's glazed with ice, and here's something that might interest you as I heat up the pot and scramble the eggs."

He hung his hat on her wall and draped his stiff sheepskin over the back of a chair as she spread a copy of the *Medicine Skull Monitor* on the table before him.

He noticed the banner headline of the extra edition before he sat down. Those Osage Police had done themselves proud down in Rawlins. They'd tailed old Marie from the county jail to a trackside shack the late Jerry Shunkaha Sapa had been holed up in. Black Wolf had gotten to be late by declining to come out with his hands up. The Osage Police had been lavish in their gratitude to wasichu sheriff's departments down yonder and up this way. As she worked at the stove with her back to him Matt Flanders said, "I never asked Ida Flint to slight anyone. I suppose that being another woman and proud of it she felt a call to sort of lay it on about *my* part in the case."

Longarm could only chuckle fondly and allow he'd noticed as he went on to read Ida's separate editorial on a woman's intuition more than making up for any lack of muscle when it came to keeping the peace.

He told Matt he didn't mind her getting that much credit, seeing he wasn't the one running for election next Tuesday. It might have hurt her self-confidence to know he'd told those fool Indians to leave his own name out of their report altogether. So he forgot to mention it.

He had to set the paper aside as she placed a big dish of ham, eggs and fried potatos in front of him, saying, "You're not the first to say that editorial could make the difference on election day. It was awfully swell of Ida to take the trouble, with all the other worries on her mind right now."

Longarm asked what the pretty little thing might be worried about. As he stuffed his hungry innards with Matt's fine cooking she told him how Ida's uncle, the job printer he had yet to meet, had failed to come home from his subscription collecting. Matt sat and poured coffee for both of them as she explained, "Ida naturally assumed he'd holed up at some spread out yonder when that blizzard hit. She didn't really start to worry until he'd failed to ride in by noon. It was going on midafternoon before she reported him missing to me. I sent some of my boys right out to search for him. Some will doubtless spend the night at outlying spreads, as we sure hope old Frank Flint did. The kids who've reported in, so far, haven't been able to come up with so much as an educated guess."

Longarm started to volunteer something dumb. Then he washed down some nice and greasy fried potatos with black coffee and agreed, "Betwixt that unexpected snow and sudden thaw an experienced tracker would have a time cutting the trail of a cavalry column out yonder."

He chewed some ham thoughtfully, and suggested, "There's this deep wooded draw, running west from that Medicine Skull Rise you mentioned."

She nodded, absently, and said, "Skeleton Wash. Why would anyone with a lick of sense head that way, day or night? It runs mostly off through Indian Reserve. So the only folk to be found along Skeleton Wash would be dead Indians."

Longarm nodded but said, "A friendly Shoshone told me why no *live* Indians cotton to that draw. Meanwhile I followed it some this afternoon to get down out of the north wind and old Frank Flint has to know the range out there better than me, right?"

Matt frowned into her coffee cup and decided, "It's worth a try if my boys can't find him somewhere more sensible. But why on earth would a man collecting from white readers want to ride off across an Indian reservation in the first place?"

Longarm answered, cautiously, "It might not have been his chosen destination. Somebody else might have taken him there, before or after."

The she-sheriff stared across the table thundergasted as Longarm insisted, "You just said he was out there all alone,

150

collecting *money,* and that's only the first motive that springs to mind when a newspaper man partial to the incumbent sheriff turns up missing just before an election. I mean to ask Miss Ida what else they might have been planning on printing about you, or anyone else."

Matt said that had been an extra edition they might not have printed if it hadn't been for that story breaking down in Rawlins. When she did agree to send some deputies along Skeleton Wash, come sunrise, he tried to keep it casual as he advised, "Have 'em look sharp at what they might take for Indian tree burials betwixt here and all them Indians we know for a fact to be dead, and Indian."

She gasped, "My Lord, you do have a vivid imagination, don't you!"

He shrugged and said, *"You'd* best send away for one, too, if you mean to make crook-catching a regular career, Miss Matt. I could tell you tales of vivid imaginations. But suffice it to say a white cadaver wrapped Cheyenne style and left in plain sight where mighty few feel like looking would be nothing next to *some* stunts I've had pulled on me."

She repressed a shudder and said, "Oh, Lord, I'd best go downstairs and leave a note on my desk. I'll have someone out to Skeleton Wash as early in the morning as possible. But Lord only knows how I'm ever going to get a wink of sleep tonight!"

Longarm didn't say anything. It wasn't for him to say. Before the sudden silence could get awkward there came a frantic pounding on the side door.

Longarm trailed along. So they were both standing there when the kid deputy called Jimmy came in, owl-eyed, to report, "It's Duke Duncan, Miss Matt. He's been drinking and reading that newspaper and cussing and drinking some more and they're afraid he's fixing to kill somebody."

Matt Flanders sighed and said, "Just let me get my hat and coat and I'll see what I can do. Is he over at the Alkali?"

Jimmy said, "He sure is, and I'd put on my gun as well if I was you, Ma'am. Duke's been cussing you specific and he don't sound too fond of Deputy Long here, neither."

151

• • •

They argued about it all the way down the stairs and then some. The night air seemed to be holding its breath, as if to keep folk from guessing it was fixing to snow some more. Even the kid deputy had strong reservations about a lady answering such an informal invitation to a gunfight in person. He said he'd heard about this mean Mex holding up in a trail town saloon with the avowed intention of gunning the next gringo who came through the swinging doors. Longarm said he'd heard right and added, "It was down in Arizona Territory and they've called that saloon the Bucket Of Blood ever since."

The she-sheriff said she was tagging along in any case. So when they got to the right dark alley mouth Longarm said, "At least let's move in sensible, Miss Matt. Why don't you and Jimmy work around to the front but stay clean across the street when you call in for him to come out. Meanwhile I'll see if I can get the drop on him from behind some bead curtains, and if there's just no nicer way . . ."

"It's my job and I mean to do any gunning that needs to be done in this county," she cut in, as if she meant it.

Longarm sighed and said, "All right. Let's send Jimmy, here, around to the front, then. There's no way at all we're going to take the man alive unless we give him the chance to surrender to *somebody*!"

She told Jimmy he'd heard Longarm. The kid didn't argue. As he moved away in the tricky light Longarm called softly after him, "Give us at least five minutes to get set up and then give us five more. It's easy to lose track of time when the times are this tense, and it's better to take too much time than not enough."

Jimmy just kept going. You couldn't see whether he was nodding or not. Longarm drew his .44-40 and growled, "All right, don't stick too tight. Make him work at hitting the both of us and if you see me going down, run like hell. In all modesty it'll mean he's too good for you."

She sighed and muttered, "Men!" as she got her own sidearm out, southpaw, and fell in to his right. He didn't ask why. The army officer in command always strode along on the right as well.

They strode along the alley crunching more cinders than they wanted to. But that couldn't be helped. The alley hadn't been cinder-paved with pussyfooting in mind. So they could only hope Duke Duncan would lay in wait for them in that saloon, the way a drunken fool was supposed to.

He didn't. Longarm shifted his six-gun to his left hand in order to shove the she-sheriff off stride into some ash cans as he fired back at someone else's muzzle flash, left-handed, and dropped out from under his hat just as a second or third wild shot hit the crown dead center.

Then their unseen ambusher had reeled through their return fusillade to crash into a fence across the alley and bounce off, cursing in confusion. So Longarm, who'd been counting, yelled, "Hold your fire, Ma'am. His gun's shot empty."

He hadn't meant for her to bound on down the alley like a catamount after a crippled deer, and he said so, loud. But then Matilda Flanders yelled, "All right, Lewis, I've had just about enough of you!" and threw a far from girlish left hook, without letting go the horse pistol in that hand.

Longarm had felt how hard the she-sheriff could punch with just her fist. So he wasn't surprised to see Duke Duncan crash through the whitewashed fence behind him and wind up on his back, half in and half out of someone's backyard.

Holstering his own gun, Longarm bent over to haul the unconscious bully out into the alley by his spurred boots, observing, "Tomorrow being a sabbath you can likely get away with holding him clean through Election Day, Ma'am. That ought to make for the fair and orderly proceedings at the polling places I was sent here to assure."

She asked, "What if he still gets enough write-in votes to win?"

To which Longarm could only reply, "In that case you and me had best be out of town before he's sworn in, Ma'am."

Then Jimmy had joined them, along with others attracted by all that gunplay. So they had plenty of help in getting Duke Duncan to the nearby jail. Nobody seemed too upset to see him arrested by a lady he'd said all those mean things about. But many seemed astounded he'd been taken alive and not even busted up too bad. So Longarm made sure everyone heard, and would likely repeat, how the pretty widow gal had taken on the self-styled hero one-on-one, and whupped his fool ass.

By the time they had Duke semiconscious but locked away for the night with plenty of those shot-up blankets it was later than some stayed up on even a Saturday night. As the crowd thinned out and Longarm found himself alone with Matt some more at the foot of those stairs it was she who murmured, "I owe you so much, Custis, and it's not as if I don't trust you, but . . ."

"It's late and folk across the way are watching," he finished for her, adding, "I finished most of that swell supper before we had to go stomp ants, Miss Matt. So I'll just be on my way and we'll say no more about it."

She said it was all right for him to drop by for breakfast, by broad day, if he liked. So they shook on it and parted friendly.

He went back to the livery, smoked a spell with the old colored cuss, and climbed back up into the hayloft to turn in sort of private again. It was warm enough up there to sleep alone, thanks to all the ponies in the stalls below. So why, he wondered, was he having so much trouble dropping off up here?

He decided it was likely that strong black coffee Matt Flanders insisted on making. He wondered if it was keeping her awake and if she felt this restless, right now.

He hoped so. He was commencing to feel she deserved to feel as restless as she had him feeling, right now.

Chapter 18

Longarm didn't have breakfast with Matt Flanders the next morning. He had some business at the telegraph office to attend to, first. He was just coming out, more free to make plans, when he heard someone call his name and turned to see that fuzzy little thing they'd called Miss Penny when she was keeping the minutes of that county meeting.

As Longarm ticked the brim of his Stetson to her she gushed about having gone over some books over and over without figuring out what he was looking for. He remembered their previous conversation just in time and told her, "That's one of the things I was looking for, Miss Penny. We uncover crooked deals by what's called a process of eliminating. If nobody's been cooking county records, there goes a whole lot of likely suspects."

She dimpled and assured him, "I was up ever so late last night, comparing the voting registers with the names printed in our county directory. Some refused to list which party they aimed to vote for. But all the folk who mean to vote next Tuesday do seem to be lawful residents. The directory was revised just last summer and . . . Have you had breakfast yet, Deputy Long?"

He sighed and confided, "To tell the pure truth it seems easier to get fed than to get washed up in this town, no offense. I just asked in the Western Union and they tell me you've no public bath in town. I know it's cold out. But I

155

can still tell I've been sleeping in Indian blankets, haylofts and such for longer than I like to go without more soap and water."

"Come on home with me, then," she cut in, latching arms with him as she insisted, "My dear old dad had modern plumbing installed before he passed away. So I've a stall shower you can use to your heart's content as, meanwhile, I'll whip you up some bacon and waffles, unless you'd rather have bacon and eggs. Then, over coffee, we can go over those books together. What do you say?"

He said yes. It would have been foolish to say anything else. The Western Union clerk had indicated that the barber charged fifteen cents for a cold bath, two bits for a hot one, and a store-bought breakfast was likely to complete the ruination of a dollar bill. For it was a tad late, already, to expect another free feed from Matt Flanders.

Fuzzy little Penelope Nelson dwelt just around the next corner behind a picket fence in, like she said, the modest but well-kept family cottage she'd inherited. The inside smelled inviting, coming in out of the cold dry November sunlight. He was glad the county paid her enough to cook with butter and indulge in real French perfume. First things coming first, he helped her out of her own coat in the hallway and hung his own hat and coat on the same elk-horn hall stand. As she led the way through dining room and kitchen to the closed in back porch he noticed how much nicer she seemed put together below her lacey choke collar. Her face might have gotten by her better if only she'd do something with that fuzzy smoke-colored hair. He suspected it was meant to stay pinned atop her head in a bun. But it never. Stray wisps busted loose in all directions to make it look as if someone had dropped a lit cheroot on her head.

As was often the case when they'd installed new plumbing in a dwelling starting out more direct, the more recent sanitary facilities were out on what had been a back porch before they'd walled it in for more warmth and privacy. It was still a shade colder and a lot more clammy, there. Penny moved over to an upright galvanized water heater standing in one corner and hunkered down in her hip-hugging skirts to strike a match, saying, "I always leave lots of kindling under fresh stovewood before I go out. There's nothing like a nice hot shower after a hard day at the office."

He mumbled something noncommittal as he stared down at her great little ass. She needed someone to tell her about her shapeless store-bought duds as well as her hopeless-looking hair. As she got a small but peppery blaze going under the water heater he tried to recall what that Miss Iris Jane had told him she used on her own spiderweby hair, aside from a touch of henna to make it more alive.

Penny rose gracefully to her feet to whip a canvas curtain out of their way to reveal the sort of dank and gloomy shower stall. He had no call to doubt her when she said there would soon be enough hot water to take the chill out of the air back here.

She suggested those waffles while he waited for all that water to heat up. While she poked up the fire in her kitchen range and whipped the batter he had plenty of time to peruse all the documents she placed before him on her kitchen table.

He tried to find something she, a professional pencil pusher, might have missed. But getting down to brass tacks he had to allow all three party machines had been playing straighter with the voters than usual. That might have been simply because it was tougher to fiddle the figures when dealing with a modest mostly rural population. Big cities were better suited to enrolling names off tombstones and declaring vacant lots or public buildings lawful places of residence.

By the time Penny wanted to serve him some breakfast he'd gone over the voting lists pretty good. So when she said she wasn't sure which party figured to win, come Tuesday, he nodded and told her, "I'd hate to have to bet a month's wages on the outcome, myself. Not knowing how all those folk registered independent are likely to swing, I'd say it was way up in the middle of the air."

As she poured the coffee she sounded worried, saying, "*Those* votes went mostly Granger, last time. I don't know what I'll do if Supervisor Burnett loses, Tuesday. I owe my job to him and his Grangers. Pappa left me a small income as well as this property, but it's not enough to make ends meet, thanks to the way prices keep rising!"

He told her no gal who made such fine waffles and swell coffee would ever starve. When he asked if she had any swains sparking her, Penny flustered and demanded, "Who'd ever look at an old maid like me, you silly?"

He said her bacon was just right, too, and added, "You can't be more than . . . say twenty-four?"

She sighed and said, "If only, bless your gallant heart. I'm closer to thirty and, as you can see, I've started to go gray already!"

There was no arguing that. So he ate some more waffles. She served him some more as she went on, uninvited, about missing the marriage boat in her misspent youth.

So he had to ask if there hadn't been anyone, at all, helping her miss boats with at least some candy, books and flowers.

She lowered her lashes and murmured, "You really know how to delve for dirty little secrets, don't you?"

When he modestly suggested that was just his job she laughed bitterly and said, "Maybe confession *is* good for the soul. Lord knows I'd die before I let anyone here in Medicine Skull find out. But what would you say about a girl, a very young girl, carrying on in secret with an older man, a dear sweet older man who meant no harm?"

Longarm replied, cautiously, "I'd say she sounded friendly. It seems a tad late to warn her she could get hurt, bad. There ought to be a law against dirty old men, however dear and sweet, taking advantage of young gals and, come to study on it, there *are.*"

He sipped more coffee and added, "None of 'em are federal, though, and since we're talking of ancient history, no offense, let's not talk about it any more, Miss Penny."

They didn't, for a spell. By the time he'd had second helpings and enjoyed a good smoke with his after-breakfast coffee, the water tank of that heater was too hot to touch, all the way up. So Longarm excused himself from his drab but gracious hostess to shut the door and shuck. He was mildly annoyed to discover no bolt on the inside of said door. As he hung his things on wall hooks he reflected that a spinster bathing or even crapping alone had less call

158

for a locked bathroom door than if she'd had a houseful of kith and kin. He knew the front and back doors of houses were bolted on the inside, with her just outside this one to scream and holler if anyone showed up with hostile intent. So he stripped to the buff and adjusted the shower to just swell before he got in, closed that curtain, and proceeded to get cleaner than he'd been for at least three gals.

The soap he found in there was strong enough to do pots and pans with, despite its fancy smell. So he was lathering himself a second time with his eyes closed when he felt a slight draft through the warm wetness and heard a familiar voice softly suggest, "I'll scrub your back if you'll scrub mine, Custis."

Naturally, he did no such thing, at first. He just set the soap aside and hauled her wet naked body closer for balance as he let the running water wash the soap from his eyes. Once it had, she looked so desirable, smiling up at him like that with her usually fuzzy hair slicked darkly down by the water splashing over both of them, that he just had to kiss her.

She kissed back, French, with little hungry-puppy noises as she ran her wet hands all over him, too. Then, as she felt him rising to the occasion between her wet soapy thighs, she gasped, "Please don't ever tell everyone I'm crazy!" and started sliding down him to wind up on her knees and kissing him French indeed.

He wedged his bare back in a corner and thrust his hips forward as he gently held her bobbing head in both hands while the warm water rained down as if to make it all seem good clean fun. As he stared down bemused at the part of her usually fuzzier hair he decided, "We ought to get you some of that hair coloring more refined ladies use and mayhap comb some Macassar pomade through it before you pin it up to go to work. You ain't a bad looking gal at all when your fright wig ain't so frightful and . . . Ah, could we finish this right, Ma'am? I'm fixing to come and I really admire the way them great thighs fork out of that trim little pelvis I was just feeling up!"

She fell back from his raging erection to sprawl wet and naked at his feet, half in and half out of the shower stall as

159

she smiled up at him with her eyes closed and husked, "Oh, yes, do it to me here and now, the way we did it *before!*"

So he dropped down to mount her slippery body, doubting she really meant him, as she wrapped wet thighs around his waist to slide her tight innards madly up and down his shaft, moaning, "Oh, Christ, Poppa, I've missed this so and I want you to really go crazy with me, now!"

So he did, albeit he wasn't sure just who might have been crazy as he made her come over and over, with her gasping some mighty odd endearments along with ingenious suggestions.

They naturally wound up in her feather bed in another part of the house after drying off pretty good on her rugs and other furniture along the way. As satisfaction and sanity began to set in he left her cooing there to go get his stuff from the bathroom. So he was sitting on the edge of the bed, lighting a cheroot, when she suddenly covered her surprisingly big tits with a rumpled pillow and sobbed, "Oh, Custis, whatever must you *think* of me?"

To which he could only reply, "For openers you're about the best lay I've had in some time and that Macassar pomade I told you about ought to do wonders for your appearance."

She looked away, blushing like the rose, to murmur, "You're great in bed and pretty, too. But the things I said, the things I *confessed* as you were doing all those dreadful things to me . . ."

He shook out his match stem and said, "I wasn't doing anything all by myself and they didn't feel so dreadful to me, honey. As for what anyone ever shouts whilst coming, nobody with a lick of sense ever holds a lover to words uttered in the heat of such moments."

She covered her face with her hands to blubber, "He warned me nobody would understand, even though we both knew our love was real and true!"

Longarm swung back into bed with her as he soothed, "What a sweet little pal might have done another time with someone else is none of my beeswax and I'll never understand why women who fuss at a man for admiring a picture in the Police Gazette insist on telling him all about every other man who's ever whistled at 'em. It ain't *romantic*, Penny. I had this one gal down in Denver ruin our romance entire by confessing to me, as if I'd asked, she'd lost her virginity to the family pet. She wanted to know if I thought her big sister, or maybe her mother, had been with that old sheep dog first, seeing it had known right off how to screw like a man, face to face."

Penny laughed incredulously and declared, "I never thought of trying it that way with a *critter* and you do raise some interesting possibilities. But you're right. It does sound sort of disgusting and I doubt I'd ever be able to own up to anything like *that*!"

He put an arm around her naked shoulders to cuddle her closer as he said, "That's what I told her. As a lawman I hear more than most about the odd family secrets best kept within the family, or, better yet, to oneself. Let's talk some more about next Tuesday. Seems to me you'll likely keep your job, seeing it's a mixed county council now. If those lists I just went over in your kitchen mean anything no single party figures to win by a landslide. Old Burnett tells me his Grangers are slipping, some, but mean to bounce back as soon as they can reorganize as a farm and labor party. I notice that county directory was typeset by old Frank Flint, or his niece. She's reported him as missing. Might be a good notion to ask her which of 'em worked most on that print job for the county."

She snuggled even closer and began to toy with the hairs on his belly as she said, "I'm sure they both worked on different pages, on and off. I've been over to that print shop many a time, dropping off or picking up other county printing. They've both been friendly and allowed me to sort of hang around when I suppose I should have been back at my desk. I know they worked together on most jobs, one setting type while the other took a breather."

He took an absent drag on his cheroot and asked what else the Flints printed for the county, observing, "Those voting lists were handwrit on business ledgers you can buy in most any stationary store."

She moved her hand lower but went on toying as she replied, "Oh, you know the sort of letterheads you see on

161

official documents, bills, business licenses and so on. What are you suggesting, now, darling? I happen to be the one they stick with all the typing. I keep carbons of all official notices, if you'd like to go over the books I've been keeping for most everyone."

He started to get rid of his smoke as she began to stroke harder down yonder. But all hell seemed to be busting loose outside and even Penny lost some interest as Longarm sat up straighter to say, "Listen. Sounds like lots of riders and a buckboard coming in over frozen mud. If we ain't having an Indian raid it's something almost as exciting and we'd best get dressed on the double."

She agreed she surely didn't want to be caught in bed on the sabbath with a gentleman caller. But Longarm still managed to get all his duds on ahead of her. So she was barefoot with her damp hair down as they parted with a kiss in her front hall. He could tell from the wistful way she buttoned his sheepskins over his gun rig for him that she might not be expecting him to kiss her anymore.

He thought about why as he eased out to the side street and then legged it faster over to the main street, where all that noise seemed to be coming from. As he joined the crowd in front of the county jail he saw a buckboard there as well, its bed empty save for some twigs and a disturbing odor. One of the she-sheriff's young deputies nodded grimly at Longarm and said, "You were on the money. We found poor old Frank pumped full of pistol rounds and wrapped up like a Cheyenne chief. He was shot from the front, close range, mayhap by someone he thought he was just talking to. Both bodies are over to the coroner's and of course Miss Matt's with Miss Ida Flint, trying to comfort the poor little thing."

Longarm was glad it hadn't been him who'd had to carry the news to the dead printer's young niece. Then he scowled at the empty wagon bed and demanded, "Did you say *bodies,* plural? I was hoping that other tree burial in Skeleton Wash might be less unusual."

Another voice in the crowd volunteered, "We figure it was that Miss Chambrun, the pretty bookkeeping gal everyone had down as running off with some passing fancy."

The first deputy said, more cautiously, "She ain't pretty, now. But wrapping her up Cheyenne style kept most of the hair on her skull and preserved the velveteen riding habit she was last seen wearing."

Someone else opined it was dumb to bundle dead folk up and stick 'em in trees where the critters couldn't get *at* 'em if one didn't want 'em identified, later.

The deputy who'd been there shrugged and said, "Oh, I don't know. Who'd have ever *looked* if Longarm, here, hadn't suggested it? The killer or killers was slick enough to use real Indian wrappings stolen from earlier sky burials. We found what was left of two Indians strewn further down the draw. But there seemed no point in hauling 'em back with us. As best we can put it together, some rascal murdered poor Miss Chambrun a spell back, noticed how good she stayed hidden in that tree, and tried the same when he, she or it murdered the poor old printer."

Before Longarm had to offer his own opinion they saw Matt Flanders and Jimmy Harper coming up the street from the Flint place. As she joined them with a weary little smile Longarm said, "I heard. Things make more sense, now."

The she-sheriff blinked and demanded, "They do? I was just telling Jimmy, here, how confounded I was, Custis. Nothing anyone else has been able to tell me makes a lick of sense to me. So tell me what you think this is all about, for Heaven's sake!"

Longarm glanced up at the sky and replied, "Not yet. I've figured out who done it. I ain't ready to make any arrests before I nail down the *motive* better. You know what they say about culling your suspects down to ability, opportunity and motive, don't you?"

She stamped a foot on the plank walk and snapped, "Damn it, Custis Long, I don't *have* any suspects, nary a one!"

He soothed for her and all to hear, "That's all right. I just told you *I* did. It's sort of complicated and I don't aim to explain over and over. So why don't you see if you can set up a meeting of the County Council and we'll want all the party chairmen there as well. That'll give me time to check just one last detail over in Skeleton Wash and if I'm

163

right I'll be proud to explain the *why* as well as the who to everyone there, see?"

She must not have. She said, "Custis, it looks like it's about to start snowing again."

Her deputy, who'd been there, offered, "We scouted for sign over yonder. I just told you we even found the original contents of them Cheyenne bundles. So what are you saying we missed?"

Longarm said, soothingly, "Nothing obvious to anyone who didn't know what he was looking for, old son. I might not even find it and it's true I could wind up riding through another blizzard on a fool's errand. But it's worth a try and I like to have everything wrapped tight when I turn a crook over to the federal prosecutor, dead or alive."

Chapter 19

It had seemed a shitty day for riding to begin with. The wind had picked up and the overcast sky was mottled with green and purple bruises by the time Longarm reined in under the wind breaking cottonwoods he'd recalled a couple of hours' ride from town.

He hadn't seen another soul on the open range as he'd made his way this far. As he dismounted and tethered that buckskin deeper in the cottonwoods, a fistful of snowflakes swirled around his head like bitty white flies.

He hauled his Winchester from its saddle boot, muttering, "I wish you wouldn't, Lord. I promised Miss Matt I'd be back in time for that meeting, just after suppertime."

The wind just moaned spooky through the bare branches overhead. But the snow didn't seem to be coming down any harder, and at this rate it seemed unlikely to stick.

He waited, smoked three widely spaced cheroots, and then waited some more. He was about to haul out a fourth when he spied movement in the tricky light to his north and quietly snicked the safety of his saddle gun instead.

Then he hunkered lower in the brushy draw to wait some more, as old T. B. Burnett and those same two bodyguards rode in, bundled up and still cussing the wind at their backs.

One of the gunslicks called, "We'd best make camp amid them cottonwoods, Boss. It's fixing to snow like hell and that draw's the best campsight for many a mile!"

Longarm had already figured that out. The county supervisor shook his head and said, "Keep going, damn it. We want to put more distance betwixt ourselves and that fool federal man before that good old blizzard sweeps our trail clean."

Longarm rose and stepped into the wagon ruts they'd been following as he said, "You boys just freeze and we'll discuss who's the fool in these parts, hear?"

They acted foolish indeed, trying to get their guns out as they wheeled their mounts to scatter, so Longarm just kept levering round after round through his Winchester's action, firing from the hip, accurate, until he'd sent all three ponies off in three directions with empty saddles.

After a hasty look-see at all three he moved back to the moaning form of T. B. Burnett, hunkered down with the warm Winchester across his thighs, and said, conversationally, "Afternoon, T. B. One of your hired guns is sincerely dead and the other's dying, spine-shot. I'd say you're done for, too, seeing I hulled you at least twice above your belt buckle."

The dying man croaked, "Who told you, you dumb son of a bitch?"

Longarm chuckled fondly and said, "You did, speaking of dumb sons of bitches."

Longarm reached for that fourth cheroot as he continued in a conversational tone, "You had me going 'til this very day. But as soon as I saw it had to be somebody who'd attend county board meetings I asked Matt Flanders to call an emergency meeting. Then I announced I'd be making an arrest or more when I got back from a tolerable ride to the north, hoping you'd beeline *south* for the nearest railroad stop, and your own guilty conscience did the rest."

"Somebody must have told you *something*." Burnett insisted, adding, "I'd moved heaven and earth to cover my tracks and I was sure I had 'em covered good!"

Longarm finished lighting his smoke, shook out the match, and said, "You didn't move all that much. You just got rid of folk who might have been getting warm and replaced 'em with less experienced help. But that in itself is what put me on to you. Any lawman who can count on his fool fingers can add up a county sheriff, a county bookkeeper and a printer who sets county documents, past and present. It was figuring the order they'd been killed in that slowed me down a mite. Other assholes with their own axes to grind didn't help."

He took a deeper drag, let it out, and confided, "I wasted time and trouble on another disgusting soul who was hoping to profit by stirring up Indian trouble. The B.I.A. can deal with him once I report him to them. I'm still working on Duke Duncan. Was he just a piss-off who'd refused to serve under a she-sheriff and figured he'd do better in her place or did you inspire him to start that sneaky write-in campaign?"

Burnett told him to go to hell.

Longarm gripped his cheroot between wolfishly bared teeth and got out his six-gun as he replied in as kindly a tone, "It's my educated opinion you'll get there first if I die this evening. I reckon I can clear up the write-in shit with a sincerely penitent Duke Duncan, if he ever expects to get out of that county jail."

Then he gently placed the muzzle of his .44-40 to the dying man's crotch and continued, "I do need your help with some other loose ends if my official report in triplicate is to make any sense at all. You're done for in any case. So making a clean breast of it can't get you hung any higher and, meanwhile, have you ever heard a man scream soprano with his balls shot off, one at a time?"

Burnett wasn't up to calling that bluff, either. So Longarm was modestly proud of the somewhat lengthly report he handed in a dozen days later, down in Denver.

Marshal Billy Vail seemed to having trouble with it, as the two of them sat in his oak-paneled office, blowing smoke at each other across Vail's cluttered desk.

Longarm didn't see why. He'd dotted every I and crossed every T before old Henry, out front, had corrected some spelling and typed it all up for him. So he said so.

Vail growled around the thick stogie he was either smoking or chewing. "I savvy most of this. There was nothing to that she-sheriff's worries about election fraud. The final count, last Tuesday, left everyone but the late T. B. Burnett in office and *he'd* have been all right if he'd just sat tight and been less murderous."

Longarm nodded and said, "That's all in there, Billy. Burnett got his job as County Supervisor in that Granger landslide of '76, and I reckon he thought the good times would roll on forever. Or mayhap he was just new at dipping into county funds because he'd never had the chance before. When a pretty good sheriff called Bob Flanders began to question items such as unrequired business licenses, Burnett had one of his hired thugs dry-gulch Flanders. He must have felt like hugging himself for being so smart when he got an inexperienced young widow appointed to serve out her dead husband's term as sheriff."

Vail nodded. "Yet she turned out better than most men might have expected, seeing how swell she did last Tuesday. I know we sort of gave her a boost by crediting her with an assist in the taking of Black Wolf, and her pistol-whipping that town bully must have gained her a vote or more. But she wasn't a stupid gal and she *was* out to get the ones who'd got her man, with the powers of her position to back her play."

Longarm shrugged and said, "She was sort of learning on the job and would have been even dumber starting out. I've dammit put down other moves he made to cover his earlier bursts of bareass greed. To begin with he started stealing a lot less greedy and making sure he left no trail on paper. He had that job printer, Frank Flint, run him off all the extra legal forms he needed to tidy up the county files. But then he naturally had to get rid of Miss Chambrun, who'd be most likely to question papers that had read another way the last time she'd seen 'em. So Burnett had his boys make her elope somewhere and replaced her with a trusted local spinster who needed the job and hadn't seen any county documents or records in their original incarnation."

Longarm smiled fondly to himself as he added, "I'm happy to say the old stockman who's replaced Burnett as county supervisor has seen fit to keep Miss Penny on and may even promote her. She seems to get on with older men."

Vail grumbled, "I ain't having trouble with Burnett's fiscal irregularities. Crooked politician is a redundancy and he'd have gotten away with his penny-ante corruption if he'd stuck to that and hadn't branched out as a bush-league butcher. Whoever heard of hiding murder victims up in trees and why did he have that printer killed with you in town and on the prod for anything the least suspicious?"

Longarm said, "Evicting a long-dead Cheyenne and wrapping a dead white gal in his place wasn't so dumb. Leaving Bob Flanders to be found on the range in such a disgusting state had stirred up a way bigger fuss than Burnett and his boys felt comfortable with. I just told you they wanted to make it look as if the Chambrun gal had just gone off on her own, alive. Anybody apt to investigate old Indian tree burials was as apt to wonder about any other kind. That shortgrass sod up yonder is mattress-thick and tougher to dig through."

He took another drag and said, "You just answered the second part of your question. I was in town on a fool's errand, thanks to you and Miss Matt Flanders, and my nosing around had Burnett worried shitless. They tried to kill me, making it look as if there was more to their she-sheriff's suspicions about election fraud than there really was. Knowing I'd question Frank Flint sooner or later, they got to him way sooner. His niece, Miss Ida, hadn't paid near as much mind to the extra forms for this and that they'd been running off for Burnett, and, anyhow, they figured that since that Chambrun gal had stayed hidden so long as a dead Indian they'd just hide Flint's cadaver the same way, and it might have worked, had not old Blake the Snake inspired a side trip I'd have never taken on my own."

Vail still looked undecided. Longarm fed some tobacco ash to the carpet mites on his side of the desk, whether they needed some or not, and insisted, "Thunderation, boss, it's all there and all the villains were acting duck soup simple. I was only running in circles a spell as each one's half-ass moves threw me off another suspect as I was getting warm. What have I left out?"

Vail smiled knowingly and asked, "You mean fit to file? I reckon we can call this a closed case, seeing nobody from this office will ever have to testify in court."

Longarm nodded and said, "Duke Duncan's been let out of jail in a chastised state. He's even offered to ride as a deputy again under a sheriff of any gender who can whip his ass. He told us one of them Allan brothers working for Burnett had encouraged him in his own dumb notions but seeing none of that matters, now, I didn't pester you or Henry with such shit in that report."

Vail nodded and said, "The B.I.A. won't more than warn that sneaky old trader, Blake, on his first attempt to get folk killed for a buck. So tell me, off the record, how well did you get to know that she-sheriff I sent you to help, in the biblical sense?"

Longarm blinked innocently and replied, "Why, Billy Vail, I never knew you expected me to get biblical with Matilda Flanders. But she was awfully pretty, as well as smart and tough. So to satisfy your curious nature, not that it's any of your damned beeswax, we did talk over country matters and we both agreed it would have been a mighty dumb indulgence with an election coming up and her and her quarters under a heap of public scrutiny."

So Billy Vail nodded and read on, knowing Longarm seldom lied outright to anyone, and it was just as well he hadn't thought to ask how Longarm had made out with a properly grateful she-sheriff *after* he'd helped her win that election.

Watch for

LONGARM ON THE DEVIL'S HIGHWAY

162nd in the bold LONGARM series
from Jove

Coming in June!

It was late afternoon when I got on my horse and rode the half mile from the house I'd built for Nora, my wife, up to the big ranch house my father and my two younger brothers still occupied. I had good news, the kind of news that does a body good, and I had taken the short run pretty fast. The two-year-old bay colt I'd been riding lately was kind of surprised when I hit him with the spurs, but he'd been lazing around the little horse trap behind my house and was grateful for the chance to stretch his legs and impress me with his speed. So we made it over the rolling plains of our ranch, the Half-Moon, in mighty good time.

I pulled up just at the front door of the big house, dropped the reins to the ground so that the colt would stand, and then made my way up on the big wooden porch, the rowels of my spurs making a *ching-ching* sound as I walked. I opened the big front door and let myself into the hall that led back to the main parts of the house.

I was Justa Williams and I was boss of all thirty-thousand deeded acres of the place. I had been so since it had come my duty on the weakening of our father, Howard, through two unforunate incidents. The first had been the early demise of our mother, which had taken it out of Howard. That had been when he'd sort of started preparing me to take over the load. I'd been a hard sixteen or a soft seventeen at the time. The next level had jumped up when he'd got nicked in the lungs by a stray bullet. After that I'd had the job of boss. The place was run with my two younger brothers, Ben and Norris.

It had been a hard job but having Howard around had made the job easier. Now I had some good news for him and I meant him to take it so. So when I went clumping back toward his bedroom that was just off the office I went to yelling, "Howard! Howard!"

He'd been laying back on his daybed, and he got up at my approach and come out leaning on his cane. He said, "What the thunder!"

I said, "Old man, sit down."

I went over and poured us out a good three fingers of whiskey. I didn't even bother to water his as I was supposed to do because my news was so big. He looked on with a good deal of pleasure as I poured out the drink. He wasn't even supposed to drink whiskey, but he'd put up such a fuss that the doctor had finally given in and allowed him one well-watered whiskey a day. But Howard claimed he never could count very well and that sometimes he got mixed up and that one drink turned into four. But, hell, I couldn't blame him. Sitting around all day like he was forced to was enough to make anybody crave a drink even if it was just for something to do.

But now he seen he was going to get the straight stuff and he got a mighty big gleam in his eye. He took the glass when I handed it to him and said, "What's the occasion? Tryin' to kill me off?"

"Hell no," I said. "But a man can't make a proper toast with watered whiskey."

"That's a fact." he said. "Now what the thunder are we toasting?"

I clinked my glass with his. I said, "If all goes well you are going to be a grandfather."

"Lord A'mighty!" he said.

We said, "Luck" as was our custom and then knocked them back.

Then he set his glass down and said, "Well, I'll just be damned." He got a satisfied look on his face that I didn't reckon was all due to the whiskey. He said, "Been long enough in coming."

I said, "Hell, the way you keep me busy with this ranch's business I'm surprised I've had the time."

"Pshaw!" he said.

We stood there, kind of enjoying the moment, and then I nodded at the whiskey bottle and said, "You keep on sneaking drinks, you ain't likely to be around for the occasion."

He reared up and said, "Here now! When did I raise you to talk like that?"

I gave him a small smile and said, "Somewhere along the line." Then I set my glass down and said, "Howard, I've got to get to work. I just reckoned you'd want the news."

He said, "Guess it will be a boy?"

I give him a sarcastic look. I said, "Sure, Howard, and I've gone into the gypsy business."

Then I turned out of the house and went to looking for our foreman, Harley. It was early spring in the year of 1898 and we were coming into a swift calf crop after an unusually mild winter. We were about to have calves dropping all over the place, and with the quality of our crossbred beef, we couldn't afford to lose a one.

On the way across the ranch yard my youngest brother, Ben, came riding up. He was on a little prancing chestnut that wouldn't stay still while he was trying to talk to me. I knew he was schooling the little filly, but I said, a little impatiently, "Ben, either ride on off and talk to me later or make that damn horse stand. I can't catch but every other word."

Ben said, mildly, "Hell, don't get agitated. I just wanted to give you a piece of news you might be interested in."

I said, "All right, what is this piece of news?"

"One of the hands drifting the Shorthorn herd got sent back to the barn to pick up some stuff for Harley. He said he seen Lew Vara heading this way."

I was standing up near his horse. The animal had been worked pretty hard, and you could take the horse smell right up your nose off him. I said, "Well, okay. So the sheriff is coming. What you reckon we ought to do, get him a cake baked?"

He give me one of his sardonic looks. Ben and I were so much alike it was awful to contemplate. Only difference between us was that I was a good deal wiser and less hotheaded and he was an even size smaller than me. He said, "I reckon he'd rather have whiskey."

I said, "I got some news for you but I ain't going to tell you now."

"What is it?"

I wasn't about to tell him he might be an uncle under such circumstances. I gave his horse a whack on the rump and said, as he went off, "Tell you this evening after work. Now get, and tell Ray Hays I want to see him later on."

He rode off, and I walked back to the ranch house thinking about Lew Vara. Lew, outside of my family, was about the best friend I'd ever had. We'd started off, however, in a kind of peculiar way to make friends. Some eight or nine years past Lew and I had had about the worst fistfight I'd ever been in. It occurred at Crook's Saloon and Cafe in Blessing, the closest town to our ranch, about seven miles away, of which we owned a good part. The fight took nearly a half an hour, and we both did our dead level best to beat the other to death. I won the fight, but unfairly. Lew had had me down on the saloon floor and was in the process of finishing me off when my groping hand found a beer mug. I smashed him over the head with it in a last-ditch effort to keep my own head on my shoulders. It sent Lew to the infirmary for quite a long stay; I'd fractured his skull. When he was partially recovered Lew sent word to me that as soon as he was able, he was coming to kill me.

But it never happened. When he was free from medical care Lew took off for the Oklahoma Territory, and I didn't hear another word from him for four years. Next time I saw him he came into that very same saloon. I was sitting at a back table when I saw him come through the door. I eased my right leg forward so as to clear my revolver for a quick draw from the holster. But Lew just came up, stuck out his hand in a friendly gesture, and said he wanted to let bygones be bygones. He offered to buy me a drink, but I had a bottle on the table so I just told him to get himself a glass and take advantage of my hospitality.

Which he did.

After that Lew became a friend of the family and was important in helping the Williams family in about three confrontations where his gun and his savvy did a good deal to turn the tide in our favor. After that we ran him against the incumbent sheriff who we'd come to dislike and no longer trust. Lew had been reluctant at first, but I'd told him that money couldn't buy poverty but it could damn well buy the sheriff's job in Matagorda County. As a result he got elected, and so far as I was concerned, he did an outstanding job of keeping the peace in his territory.

Which wasn't saying a great deal because most of the trouble he had to deal with, outside of helping us, was the occasional Saturday night drunk and the odd Main Street dogfight.

So I walked back to the main ranch house wondering what he wanted. But I also knew that if it was in my power to give, Lew could have it.

I was standing on the porch about five minutes later when he came riding up. I said, "You want to come inside or talk outside?"

He swung off his horse. He said, "Let's get inside."

"You want coffee?"

"I could stand it."

"This going to be serious?"

"Is to me."

"All right."

I led him through the house to the dining room, where we generally, as a family, sat around and talked things out. I said, looking at Lew, "Get started on it."

He wouldn't face me. "Wait until the coffee comes. We can talk then."

About then Buttercup came staggering in with a couple of cups of coffee. It didn't much make any difference about what time of day or night it was, Buttercup might or might not be staggering. He was an old hand of our father's who'd helped to develop the Half-Moon. In his day he'd been about the best horse breaker around, but time and tumbles had taken their toll. But Howard wasn't a man to forget past loyalties so he'd kept Buttercup on as a cook.

His real name was Butterfield, but me and my brothers had called him Buttercup, a name he clearly despised, for as long as I could remember. He was easily the best shot with a long-range rifle I'd ever seen. He had an old .50-caliber Sharps buffalo rifle, and even with his old eyes and seemingly unsteady hands he was deadly anywhere up to five hundred yards. On more than one occasion I'd had the benefit of that seemingly ageless ability. Now he set the coffee down for us and give all the indications of making himself at home. I said, "Buttercup, go on back out in the kitchen. This is a private conversation."

I sat. I picked up my coffee cup and blew on it and then took a sip. I said, "Let me have it, Lew."

He looked plain miserable. He said, "Justa, you and your family have done me a world of good. So has the town and the county. I used to be the trash of the alley and y'all helped bring me back from nothing." He looked away. He said, "That's why this is so damn hard."

"What's so damned hard?"

But instead of answering straight out he said, "They is going to be people that don't understand. That's why I want you to have the straight of it."

I said, with a little heat, "Goddammit, Lew, if you don't tell me what's going on I'm going to stretch you out over that kitchen stove in yonder."

He'd been looking away, but now he brought his gaze back to me and said, "I've got to resign, Justa. As sheriff. And not only that, I got to quit this part of the country."

Thoughts of his past life in the Oklahoma Territory flashed through my mind, when he'd been thought an outlaw and later proved innocent. I thought maybe that old business had come up again and he was going to have to flee for his life and his freedom. I said as much.

He give me a look and then made a short bark that I reckoned he took for a laugh. He said, "Naw, you got it about as backwards as can be. It's got to do with my days in the Oklahoma Territory all right, but it ain't the law. Pretty much the opposite of it. It's the outlaw part that's coming to plague me."

180

It took some doing, but I finally got the whole story out of him. It seemed that the old gang he'd fallen in with in Oklahoma had got wind of his being the sheriff of Matagorda County. They thought that Lew was still the same young hellion and that they had them a bird nest on the ground, what with him being sheriff and all. They'd sent word that they'd be in town in a few days and they figured to "pick the place clean." And they expected Lew's help.

"How'd you get word?"

Lew said, "Right now they are raising hell in Galveston, but they sent the first robin of spring down to let me know to get the welcome mat rolled out. Some kid about eighteen or nineteen. Thinks he's tough."

"Where's he?"

Lew jerked his head in the general direction of Blessing. "I throwed him in jail."

I said, "You got me confused. How is you quitting going to help the situation? Looks like with no law it would be even worse."

He said, "If I ain't here maybe they won't come. I plan to send the robin back with the message I ain't the sheriff and ain't even in the county. Besides, there's plenty of good men in the county for the job that won't attract the riffraff I seem to have done." He looked down at his coffee as if he was ashamed.

I didn't know what to say for a minute. This didn't sound like the Lew Vara I knew. I understood he wasn't afraid and I understood he thought he was doing what he thought was the best for everyone concerned, but I didn't think he was thinking too straight. I said, "Lew, how many of them is there?"

He said, tiredly, "About eighteen all told. Counting the robin in the jail. But they be a bunch of rough hombres. This town ain't equipped to handle such. Not without a whole lot of folks gettin' hurt. And I won't have that. I figured on an argument from you, Justa, but I ain't going to make no battlefield out of this town. I know this bunch. Or kinds like them." Then he raised his head and give me a hard look. "So I don't want no argument out of you. I come out to tell you what was what because I care about what you

181

might think of me. Don't make me no mind about nobody else but I wanted you to know."

I got up. I said, "Finish your coffee. I got to ride over to my house. I'll be back inside of half an hour. Then we'll go into town and look into this matter."

He said, "Dammit, Justa, I done told you I—"

"Yeah, I know what you told me. I also know it ain't really what you want to do. Now we ain't going to argue and I ain't going to try to tell you what to do, but I am going to ask you to let us look into the situation a little before you light a shuck and go tearing out of here. Now will you wait until I ride over to the house and tell Nora I'm going into town?"

He looked uncomfortable, but, after a moment, he nodded. "All right," he said. "But it ain't going to change my mind none."

I said, "Just go in and visit with Howard until I get back. He don't get much company and even as sorry as you are you're better than nothing."

That at least did make him smile a bit. He sipped at his coffee, and I took out the back door to where my horse was waiting.

Nora met me at the front door when I came into the house. She said, "Well, how did the soon-to-be grandpa take it?"

I said, "Howard? Like to have knocked the heels off his boots. I give him a straight shot of whiskey in celebration. He's so damned tickled I don't reckon he's settled down yet."

"What about the others?"

I said, kind of cautiously, "Well, wasn't nobody else around. Ben's out with the herd and Norris is in Blessing. Naturally Buttercup is drunk."

Meanwhile I was kind of edging my way back toward our bedroom. She followed me. I was at the point of strapping on my gunbelt when she came into the room. She said, "Why are you putting on that gun?"

It was my sidegun, a .42/40-caliber Colts revolver that I'd been carrying for several years. I had two of them, one that I wore and one that I carried in my saddlebags. The

182

gun was a .40-caliber chambered weapon on a .42-caliber frame. The heavier frame gave it a nice feel in the hand with very little barrel deflection, and the .40-caliber slug was big enough to stop any thing you could hit solid. It had been good luck for me and the best proof of that was that I was alive.

I said, kind of looking away from her, "Well, I've got to go into town."

"Why do you need your gun to go into town?"

I said, "Hell, Nora, I never go into town without a gun. You know that."

"What are you going into town for?"

I said, "Norris has got some papers for me to sign."

"I thought Norris was already in town. What does he need you to sign anything for?"

I kind of blew up. I said, "Dammit, Nora, what is with all these questions? I've got business. Ain't that good enough for you?"

She give me a cool look. "Yes," she said. "I don't mess in your business. It's only when you try and lie to me. Justa, you are the worst liar in the world."

"All right," I said. "All right. Lew Vara has got some trouble. Nothing serious. I'm going to give him a hand. God knows he's helped us out enough." I could hear her maid, Juanita, banging around in the kitchen. I said, "Look, why don't you get Juanita to hitch up the buggy and you and her go up to the big house and fix us a supper. I'll be back before dark and we'll all eat together and celebrate. What about that?"

She looked at me for a long moment. I could see her thinking about all the possibilities. Finally she said, "Are you going to run a risk on the day I've told you you're going to be a father?"

"Hell no!" I said. "What do you think? I'm going in to use a little influence for Lew's sake. I ain't going to be running any risks."

She made a little motion with her hand. "Then why the gun?"

"Hell, Nora, I don't even ride out into the pasture without a gun. Will you quit plaguing me?"

It took a second, but then her smooth, young face calmed down. She said, "I'm sorry, honey. Go and help Lew if you can. Juanita and I will go up to the big house and I'll personally see to supper. You better be back."

I give her a good, loving kiss and then made my adieus, left the house, and mounted my horse and rode off.

But I rode off with a little guilt nagging at me. I swear, it is hell on a man to answer all the tugs he gets on his sleeve. He gets pulled first one way and then the other. A man damn near needs to be made out of India rubber to handle all of them. No, I wasn't riding into no danger that March day, but if we didn't do something about it, it wouldn't be long before I would be.

Explore the exciting Old West with
one of the men who made it wild!

A special offer for people who enjoy reading the best Westerns published today.

WESTERNS!

NO OBLIGATION

Mail the coupon below

To start your subscription and receive 2 FREE WESTERNS, fill out the coupon below and mail it today. We'll send your first shipment which includes 2 FREE BOOKS as soon as we receive it.

Mail To: **True Value Home Subscription Services, Inc. P.O. Box 5235**
120 Brighton Road, Clifton, New Jersey 07015-5235

YES! I want to start reviewing the very best Westerns being published today. Send me my first shipment of 6 Westerns for me to preview FREE for 10 days. If I decide to keep them, I'll pay for just 4 of the books at the low subscriber price of $2.75 each; a total $11.00 (a $21.00 value). Then each month I'll receive the 6 newest and best Westerns to preview Free for 10 days. If I'm not satisfied I may return them within 10 days and owe nothing. Otherwise I'll be billed at the special low subscriber rate of $2.75 each; a total of $16.50 (at least a $21.00 value) and save $4.50 off the publishers price. There are never any shipping, handling or other hidden charges. I understand I am under no obligation to purchase any number of books and I can cancel my subscription at any time, no questions asked. In any case the 2 FREE books are mine to keep.

Name

Street Address   Apt. No.

City   State   Zip Code

Telephone

Signature
(if under 18 parent or guardian must sign)

Terms and prices subject to change. Orders subject
to acceptance by True Value Home Subscription
Services, Inc.

515-10849-9